Projec   ...ion: Reentry

Book 2

All Rights Reserved

Copyright © 2019 Heather Carson

Courtesy of Blue Tuesday Books

ISBN: 9781702099431

Project Dandelion: Reentry

Heather Carson

"Get to the cabin."

The words of Katrina's father echo in her mind. One sentence, her sole purpose…

Chapter 1

Two weeks was all it took. Two weeks for the whole world to change. The sky went dark. Not dark as night, but dark as in devoid of life. Blue gave way to shades of grey and the sun burned red as if in pain. The air hung heavy like the burning of a million oil fields. White ash mummified everything that didn't run when the fallout came.

Fourteen days, Katrina thought. It didn't seem that many when you counted them, but fourteen days felt like a lifetime within the shelter. A lot could happen in two weeks.

Katrina glanced at the rearview mirror. She saw the dust that the old Chevy truck she was driving kicked up from the dirt road. In the bottom corner of the mirror, she could see Dreya and Jayden leaning against one another in the bed of the truck. Their hazmat suits were still intact. Inside the cab, Dreya's little sister Mia sat sandwiched between Katrina and James. The windows were closed so the three of them had taken off their masks. All five of them had been selected to survive with a group of other teenagers in an underground government designed fallout shelter when the world fell apart during a nuclear war. Now they were running away from the shelter and the society that the remaining kids had built there. The plan was to head to Katrina's cabin in the mountains that her father had stocked with survival gear.

"Do you think the whole world looks like this?" Mia asked while grimly watching the horizon. "Is it all this empty?"

Katrina laughed. "I sure hope not. We are still in a pretty remote area of the desert. Once we get to some civilization, I hope it will look much different." Katrina turned to smile at James over Mia's head, but he was staring out the window.

Last night, they had camped on the concrete slab platform where their parents had dropped them off at hours before the bombs dropped. They were given sleeping pills and transported from the platform on a bus to the shelter which was sealed off until the air quality levels were safer. Thankfully, it had only been two weeks. Katrina shuddered to think about what would have happened had it been longer.

They sat around the fire that evening eating packages of their saved food. Dreya told Katrina that she and Mia had never been to this area before. They were from a coastal city in Delaware and were vacationing in Lake Tahoe when a man in a suit approached their parents at the hotel restaurant. They were put into their rental car and left for the platform minutes later. Katrina thought they were lucky because she couldn't imagine how those major metropolitan areas looked now. Jayden lived more local. His family was from outside of Las Vegas and his dad was the elected sheriff of their county.

Katrina glanced up at the mirror again and saw Jayden put his arm over Dreya's shoulders. Dreya didn't flinch like she did when Lark tried the same thing in the shelter. Ugh Lark, Katrina thought. She was glad to be getting as far away as possible from that guy and his wacky politics. Not wacky, dangerous. The rest of the kids that were following his vision would be in for a rude awakening soon. Katrina unconsciously pressed the gas pedal a little harder.

"How far until we reach the next town?" James asked startling Katrina from her train of thought.

"Just a couple of hours. These roads aren't major highways, but we will hit about three towns if I take the direct route and only one if I take some back roads."

"How many houses along the way?" He turned to face her. Katrina glanced over to see his eyes staring through her, a shade of murky blue, which she had learned would happen when he was thinking something through.

"Not many." She looked out the windshield again. "A trailer here and there. The town is a small one too. Population less than 2,000 or something."

"Is there no way to avoid it?" James asked.

"Not really but I'm not too worried. These are farmers and in this rural area they may have been able to avoid a lot of the destruction." Katrina smiled at James, but he didn't return the gesture. "We can scope it out first if that makes you feel more comfortable."

James nodded his head. "Where is the gun?"

Mia's eyes opened wide as she alternated looking at the two of them. "What gun?" she whispered.

Katrina raised her eyebrows. "What makes you think there is a gun?"

"Oh come on," James finally laughed. "Your dad is a prepper who stocked a cabin in the mountains just in case the world ended. He somehow left this truck for you in the event that he wouldn't be back to get you when the doors opened, and you'd have to get to the cabin by yourself. Plus, he is a Marine right?" His smile broadened. "Of course he left you a gun."

Katrina grinned. "It's behind your seat." James nodded and went back to looking out the window.

Chapter 2

"Wait." Mia's eyes were as big as saucers. "There is a gun in here. Why do we need a gun? Do you even know how to shoot a gun?"

Katrina smiled at the girl. "Yes, I know how to shoot. It's here in case we ever need to use it. Let's just hope that we never have to."

Before they crested the ridge over the town, James pointed to a dirt turnoff on a hill that overlooked the valley. Katrina parked the truck at the base of the hill and the three of them put on their masks before climbing out. The Personal Radiation Emergency Monitor device on their suits read the air radiation levels as high. Jayden and Dreya jumped out of the back of the truck.

Mia ran up to her sister. "Dreya there is a gun in the truck!"

"Does that really surprise you?" Dreya patted her sister on the head with her gloved hand. "I mean there were 9,000 nuclear weapons deployed targeting all the major cities in the world which probably wiped out most of the population. A single gun doesn't seem that scary now, does it?"

James started climbing the hill. "I'm going to check out this town we are about to drive through."

Katrina followed him up with Jayden, Dreya, and Mia close behind. They laid on their stomachs at the top of the hill which gave them an eagle view of the valley below. James pointed out the tire spike strips along the road. There were people moving about the center of the town. They had blankets over their heads with gas or surgical masks tied across their faces. The people were busy cleaning up debris from the main street. Ash coated all the houses making it seem as though snow had fallen in summer. The roads around the main streets had been barricaded off and large metal fencing laced with barbwire surrounded the town.

The five of them slowly shimmied back down the hill.

"We need to go around," James said to Katrina as they reached the truck.

"The only way to do that is to off road through this desert and we are low on gas as it is. If we get lost, we might get stuck somewhere and have to hike out. I think they will let us through. All of that is just a deterrent to people who want to hurt them," Katrina said.

"It's a whole lot safer if we don't test that theory out," Jayden sided with James.

Dreya looked at her little sister before turning to Katrina. "How positive are you that it will be okay?"

"Betting odds?" Katrina asked. "Not the greatest but I don't see another way. We have enough gas as it is to get to the cabin as long as we don't waste it. Plus, a part of me thinks we will have an advantage because we are just a group of kids. They might take pity on us or realize that there isn't anything to be afraid of. Then again, they might be scared and scared people don't think straight."

"I don't want to take the chance. Maybe if we had more guns for back up and the streets weren't barricaded. But this plan is too risky." James shook his head.

"I guess we could go around, but it is going to be a bumpy ride." Katrina shrugged. "As long as you are all okay with us hiking out when we run out of gas."

Dreya nodded. "I'd rather take the safest odds right now even if it is the harder road."

"Um, guys," Mia interrupted their deliberations. "I don't think that it will matter what we decide on in about 30 seconds." Katrina looked up to see three pickup trucks closing in on them from behind.

Chapter 3

The trucks were coming in fast, leaving a cloud of blinding dust and ash in their wake. Two of the trucks were dark grey, a Ford and a crew cab Dodge, and one was a bright blue lifted Toyota. From what Katrina could see, there were at least two men riding inside of each truck with the passengers holding a shotgun across their chest. There were two more men standing in the back of each truck leaning against the roof with rifles pointed directly at the kids.

"Is it time to pull that gun out yet?" Mia asked in a panic.

"Definitely not," Katrina said as she blew out a steadying breath. "Walk away from the truck slowly with your hands in the air." Katrina put her hands up and began walking forward with Dreya and Mia following behind her.

Jayden stood whistling as he leaned against the truck with his back towards the patrol. James quickly saw what he was about to do so he raised his arms and stepped behind Jayden, momentarily shielding him from the view of the vehicles approaching. Jayden slid his hand into his bag in the truck bed and pulled out a piece of the sink piping they had dismantled in the shelter before leaving. In one fluid motion, he unzipped his suit, slid the pipe inside of it, and rezipped it before turning around slowly with his hands in the air to walk behind James.

They stepped ten feet away from the Chevy and stood in a line facing the oncoming trucks. Katrina dropped to her knees in the dirt. Her four friends did the same.

"Still betting that they are harmless?" Dreya asked Katrina.

"Right now, I am praying," she answered.

The trucks slowed down as they came to a stop forming a half circle around the teens with all of the guns pointed at them. The men began to yell "don't move". A burly man with a bandana over his mouth that barely covered his red beard jumped out of the back of the Ford truck. From his backpack, he pulled out a bag of zip ties and ran up to secure each of the kids' hands starting with Jayden. Once their wrists were bound, the driver of the Dodge stepped out.

The Dodge driver was in his mid-thirties and had an old military gas mask strapped across his face. His hair was buzzed short and he wore a mechanics t-shirt advertising a local business. He walked right up to Katrina and tilted her head back to see inside her mask. Then he did the same to the rest of them.

"They are only kids," Buzzcut yelled back to the trucks.

"Yeah, but they were watching the town," Redbeard called back. "And check out those suits they are wearing. Something's off about this."

Two more men got down from the trucks and went to check out the Chevy. They pulled out Jayden's open bag from the back and emptied it onto the ground. The wool blanket, cleaning solution bottle filled with water, rope made from sheets, and the dehydrated food packs from the MREs they were fed in the shelter fell out onto the dirt.

One of the men grabbed the bag itself, which was made of plastic mattress liner and woven through with strips of torn sheet, to show the other man. He raised his eyebrows. "What is this? Did you make these? Where are you from?" He quickly scooped up the rest of the packs and emptied them out letting the contents litter the desert floor.

Before Katrina could respond, Buzzcut said, "Those are military food rations. Are you guys with the government?" All the men immediately pointed their guns back at the kids and began yelling at them.

Dreya yelled back, "No! We aren't. We don't even know what is happening. We have literally been trapped in an underground shelter for two weeks. Our parents just dropped us off there and we left as soon as the doors opened."

Katrina cringed. Too much, Dreya! There was something that she wasn't understanding, and she wanted to wait for the men to talk more to get the answers.

"Stop talking," Buzzcut told the men behind him. "Let her speak. What did you just say?"

Katrina interjected, "She was trying to say we are hungry and confused. We don't know where we are. We saw your town, but we didn't want to just drive up in case you were dangerous."

"Yeah, that's very obvious," Buzzcut said. "But I want to hear what she was saying." He pointed to Dreya. "What did you say about your parents dropping you off and the doors opening?" Dreya froze. Katrina could see the gears turning in Buzzcut's head.

"Oh shit." Buzzcut's eyes widened. "They are Project Dandelion." The men grew silent as they looked to one another.

"What do we do boss?" a skinny guy in the back of the Toyota asked.

Buzzcut ran his hand over the stubbled hair on his head. "I don't know."

"Wait," Katrina said. "We don't know what that even means. We aren't a part of project anything. We have just been in a fallout shelter for two weeks…"

"Shut up," Buzzcut interrupted her.

"Let's just shoot them," Redbeard said. "Screw their project and screw the government. Send them a message by getting rid of these kids."

"Oh come on man," James called out as Dreya scooted closer to her sister. "We don't even know what you are talking about and we haven't done anything wrong."

"Stop moving," Buzzcut yelled. "I'm trying to think."

"Just get rid of them," another guy shouted. "What if they are looking for them? We don't need to draw any attention to ourselves."

"Who are they and what do they care about us?" Katrina asked the man in the truck. He spit on the ground in reply. The men were growing restless as they shifted around while holding their guns. Katrina racked her brain trying to think of a way to diffuse the situation before they ended up dying right there in the desert.

"I vote shoot them," a third man called out and more began to agree. Katrina started to take off her mask hoping that seeing the face of a teenage girl kneeling there might prevent them from actually taking the shot.

"Enough," Buzzcut put his hand up. "We are going to keep them as hostages. That gives us a card to play if they come through. We'll sell them if we need to or we can kill them later if they don't end up serving a purpose."

"What?" Jayden and James yelled out simultaneously and Buzzcut pointed his shotgun toward them.

"Sit down boys," he said. "You aren't dying today." James and Jayden got back down to their knees. "Throw them in the back of their truck. Gene can drive it into town." Redbeard, aka Gene, climbed into the driver's seat of Katrina's Chevy as six men ran over to get the teens into the truck bed. They grabbed them by the back of their suits and roughly lifted them in the back before closing the tailgate. One man came over with a duffle bag which he used to pick up the discarded contents of the kids' packs.

Mia scooted across the lining of the truck bed to sit next to her sister as Katrina struggled to sit up from lying on her stomach. James rolled to the back near the rear window and Jayden slid across next to him as the truck started moving. The men ran back to their own trucks and they all pulled onto the dirt road which headed toward the highway. Katrina locked eyes with Jayden just as he put the exposed tail of the zip tie in his teeth and pulled it as tightly as he could. Turning to her side, she lifted her hands to her mouth and did the same.

The truck picked up speed and the kids began to bounce around in the back with each rut that Gene hit. Katrina finally got into a seated position. She looked over to see James and Jayden furiously shouting at one another, but she couldn't hear what they were saying through the deafening roar of the wind as the truck peeled out onto the main road. Behind her, the three trucks following spread out to flank them on either side.

Jayden put his hands on Dreya and Mia's shoulders, pushing them down so they lay flat against the truck bed floor. Then he unzipped his suit and reached in to pull out the metal pipe. He kept his body slightly turned from the view of the following trucks and laid the pipe across his leg. Katrina registered what they were about to do just as James and Jayden nodded to each other.

Time slowed down as Katrina watched Jayden lift his arms over his head. James motioned toward the driver's seat and Katrina nodded to him. Jayden slammed his wrists into the middle of his body and the zip tie broke in two. He swiftly grabbed the metal pipe as Katrina lifted her own arms up and tried to break free. It took her three times before she was able to get the zip tie to snap.

Jayden smashed the back window with the pipe. The glass exploded into a shower of jagged marbles and ice chunks that spilled into the cab and back of the truck. Katrina pressed her body to the floor as the shots began to fire from the three trucks behind them. Gene turned around just as James used his zip tied hands to pull him out of the driver's seat by his neck through the broken window. Jayden reached behind the passenger seat to pull out the rifle and then he also dropped to the floor.

Katrina took a deep breath before she scrambled across the bed of the truck. James had just finished wrestling Gene out of the cab as Katrina climbed through the busted window and slipped behind the wheel. The truck was beginning to slow down but she slammed on the gas pedal as more bullets peppered the vehicle. The windshield burst, covering her lap with glass. She pulled the wheel hard to the right. The momentum helped James as he finished pushing Gene over the edge and out onto the road. The men in the Ford stopped to pick him up.

Katrina pulled down the seat in the cab to expose the center console. She opened it quickly with one hand and retrieved the box of bullets which she handed back through the broken window to Jayden. She kept the accelerator pressed to the floor and moments later the sound of the rifle being shot from the back of the truck filled the cab. Jayden expertly shot out the tires on the grey Dodge and blue Toyota. She drove the truck through the desert as they passed wide around the border of the town. The teens bounced around in a bed of glass and Katrina didn't slow down until that awful place was miles away from the sight of her cracked rearview mirror.

Chapter 4

As they crested another hill in the middle of the desert about three hours away from the town, Katrina came to a stop. The adrenaline from the earlier events was beginning to wear off and she was starving. Plus, she wanted to check on her friends. She scanned the horizon and still couldn't see anyone following them.

Katrina opened the driver's side door and glass came pouring out onto the ground. She carefully stepped down and tried wiping the rest of the glass off the seat with her gloved hand. Jayden dropped the tailgate as Dreya and Mia used their feet to push out more glass from the back. Katrina heard the crunch of James' footsteps as he walked through the shards of glass to stand behind her. He wrapped his arms around her, and she stopped sweeping to put her hands on his forearms.

"Are you okay?" he asked.

Katrina tensed. "Yes. Why wouldn't I be okay?" She turned around to face him. James stared at her with his eyebrow raised before he started laughing. A second later, Katrina burst out laughing too.

Mia stopped sweeping when she heard them. "Are you guys seriously making jokes right now?" She put her hands up in the air. "Hello, we almost died. There is absolutely nothing funny about this. You are both freaks." Dreya turned to look at Jayden and they both also began to laugh. Mia put her hands on top of her head. "Great. I'm surrounded by freaks."

Katrina almost fell over because she was laughing so hard. James caught her. As she tried to stand up, she realized she couldn't put all her weight on her right leg. She froze and looked up at James. They both looked down at her leg and saw that her suit was torn and bloody.

"You are hurt." James stopped laughing as he picked Katrina up and carried her over to the back of the truck.

"I'm fine," Katrina said as he sat her down on the tailgate. "It's probably just a scrape."

"What's going on?" Dreya asked as she jumped down from the truck. Katrina tried to say "nothing", but James cut her off.

"She's hurt. Her leg is bleeding." James began to unzip her suit.

"I'm not a child," Katrina said while pushing his hand away. She pulled off her own suit and shivered when the air hit her skin feeling unnaturally exposed. Then she lifted the leg of her ripped and soaking sweatpants to see a deep gash in her calf.

Dreya walked closer to her. "Can I take a look?" Katrina nodded and then winced when Dreya delicately touched her knee. "This is going to need stiches. Crap. We have to find a needle and thread. First, let's do something to stop the bleeding." James began to hurriedly unzip his own suit.

"Um. What are you doing dude?" Katrina asked him.

"Taking off my shirt so we have something to wrap around the wound," he answered.

"Gross. I don't need your sweaty shirt," Katrina laughed. "There is some gauze in the emergency bag behind the front seat."

Mia pulled out the bag which held gauze, ace wraps, some medicine, a flashlight, lighters, bottled water, and a couple of MRE packs. "Geez. Anything else in here?" she asked handing the bag over. "All that is missing is a radio and a spaceship to get us off the planet."

Katrina smiled. "I'm not sure that would fit. But there is a utility knife and Chapstick in the glovebox, jumper cables under the seat, and I'm sure there is a small axe floating around in there somewhere." Her friends stared at her and Katrina shrugged. "My dad is a prepper, remember?"

"Alright, well hopefully there are some antibiotics in the med pouch, but we still need a needle to sew you up."

"There are a few houses on the way to the cabin. I don't want to risk going through any more towns though. And there are medical supplies at the cabin too," Katrina said.

"I agree with the avoiding towns part. How long until we get to the cabin?" Dreya asked.

"Well, whenever we find the main road which I think is about 30 minutes that way," Katrina pointed northeast, "it should be around a 6-hour drive."

"I think we will do okay for about 6 hours," Dreya said.

"Except we are going to run out of gas well before we get there. Unless we find a town to fill up in, we are going to have to hike in." Katrina gave Dreya a strained smile.

"Okay." Dreya exhaled. She looked to her sister before turning back to Katrina. "How long of a hike?"

"A week or two?" Katrina answered. "We will have to cut through the mountains because it would be too risky walking night and day along the main roads." Katrina saw the worry in Dreya's eyes. "Is this still okay?"

"Do we have another option?" Dreya asked.

"Not really. I don't know what those guys were talking about or why they were so afraid of the government, but I don't want to ever risk being held as a hostage again. I just want to get to the cabin. No one knows it is there besides me and my dad and there are enough supplies there to live comfortably for a few years. Getting to the cabin is my main priority right now."

"It's mine too," James said. "Except you're not going to be able to hike with your leg like this."

"I'll be okay," Katrina said staring at him.

"Why don't we find somewhere to get supplies soon then?" Dreya said. "We need you to be able to walk if we are all going to make it to the cabin."

Dreya took over driving the truck while Katrina sat with her leg elevated on top of James' lap in the back. Now that all the adrenaline had worn off, Katrina realized how much pain she was really in. She was reminded of it every time Dreya hit a bump. Thankfully, they found the main road fast and it was a much smoother drive. Jayden sat in the back with them watching the world pass by.

"Where'd you learn to shoot like that?" Katrina shouted to him over the wind.

"I've been shooting since I was a kid," Jayden called back. "Though I've never shot a car before. Well, at least not a moving car." Katrina smiled and told him that she was grateful he had come along. He nodded and turned back to look at the desert.

An hour or so later, the scenery began to change. There were outcroppings of large rock formations. Further down the road, pine trees began to appear sparsely throughout the horizon. Before they went over the next hill, Katrina asked James to tap Dreya's shoulder so that she would pull over.

*

"There are a couple of trailers down in this next valley. We are going to split from the main highway and take a side road up that mountain there," Katrina told everyone as she pointed east. "The road that we need to be on will take us behind the houses. I guess if no one is there then we can stop for supplies."

"I think that's a good idea," James said. "It will be fast, in and out. Jayden and I will go."

Katrina rolled her eyes. "Why just the guys, huh? Don't think the girls are fast enough?" she asked sarcastically.

"Let's see." James looked straight through her. "Dreya is driving and needs to stay ready in case we need to get away quickly. Mia stays with her and you are a cripple right now." Katrina tried to respond but James interrupted. "Now isn't the time to question gender stereotypes. This is the time to shut up and say thank you."

Katrina folded her arms across her chest as she muttered "thank you."

They descended into the valley and Katrina saw the four trailers spread out on their uneven plots of land just as her memory had left them. There were no signs of life. No car tracks in the ash that covered the smaller roads leading into the driveways. They picked the house that was closest to the turnoff road they needed to take. Dreya drove slowly into the front yard. Katrina watched for any movement in the house and saw nothing. There was a Jeep parked on the gravel driveway. The driver side door was left open. Ash covered the inside of the door and the seat.

"Looks like no one is home," Jayden said as he grabbed the rifle and stood up. James also stood and turned to wink at Katrina. She huffed at him, but her heart was beating hard in her chest as she watched them climb out of the truck. Dreya turned the vehicle around and Katrina scooted forward to drop the tailgate in case they needed to jump back in fast. James knocked on the door as Jayden stood point with the rifle. When no one answered, James turned the door knob. The house was unlocked. He waved at Katrina before walking inside. Jayden followed him in.

Katrina held her breath and started slowly counting to herself. She could see through the dirty windows with lace valence curtains as the guys rummaged around the living room. They disappeared from her line of sight and she continued counting. Seventy-four, seventy-five, seventy-six…

Jayden and James came running out of the door. They each wore a back pack and carried blankets in one arm. James had a fly-fishing rod sticking up high out of his bag like a flag and in his free hand he carried a pistol. Jayden balanced two jugs of water in the crook of his elbow. They slung the gear into the truck and Jayden ran to the side of the house to unscrew the hose from the spigot. He cut off a large piece and ran back to the Jeep. James pulled an empty gas can out from the back of the vehicle. Katrina watched as they tried to syphon gas from the Jeep's gas tank, but nothing came out. James shook his head and the boys ran back to the truck.

Katrina pulled the tailgate up once they were in and Dreya started to drive away. James was staring at the sky, his face serious. "What happened?" Katrina asked.

"They shot them," James answered bluntly. "Someone shot them in their own house. The place was a disaster and I took the gun from the man's hands. Just an old man and his wife. They were left lying there on their kitchen floor."

Katrina moved closer to him and wrapped her hand around his. "Thank you for going in there for me," she told him.

He nodded and put his arm over her shoulders.

Chapter 5

Behind them was the desert and in front of them was the base of the mountain range that stretched forever in either direction. The main road they crossed had been traveled on recently from what Katrina could tell. A light dusting of ash covered multiple deep track marks. Katrina felt uneasy and told Dreya to pull over.

"We need to get off this road," Katrina told her friends as they huddled against the shot out window. "How much gas do we have left?"

Dreya let go of the steering wheel and tried to smooth down the crazy mess of flyaways in her braid. She settled on tucking the loose hair behind her ears. "Not much," she said. "We'll be driving on fumes soon."

"Crap," Katrina sighed. "Alright. The plan is to take that steep road over there. Let's get as high up the mountain as we can before we have to go on foot." Dreya nodded and started the engine.

As they drove up the hill, Katrina thought back to her childhood memories tied to the old truck. She remembered her father driving them home late one winter night. A light rain had started which quickly turned into fat snowflakes. The snow melted so fast against the speeding truck that it looked as if they were shooting through the stars. Her dad had taught her how to change the oil and the tires on the truck one summer day when she was twelve. She learned to drive in this truck. Katrina shook her head. She was getting too sentimental. It's just a vehicle, she thought.

Her ears started to pop, and it brought her out of her thoughts. Glancing around, she saw everyone trying to yawn or yanking on their earlobes to relieve the pressure. They were more than halfway up the mountain. Come on old girl, Katrina touched the side of the truck. Get us a little bit farther.

At 8,000ft the truck started slipping. Dreya turned it to the side of the road and pulled the emergency brake. "That's it," Dreya called over her shoulder. "There's nothing left."

"That's fine," Katrina said as she dropped the tailgate again. "We got further than I thought we would. Now it's time to hike."

"Why don't we get you stitched up first?" James said while helping Katrina get down from the truck.

"Not right now," Katrina said. She winced as she landed on her right foot. "I want to get off the road and up to that vantage point over there first so we can see if anyone is coming."

Katrina limped over to the front of the truck and pulled the seat forward. She grabbed the emergency pack and put the extra bullets, road flares, and hatchet into the bag. Then she slid the seat back and opened the center console to get the utility knife, flashlight, and lighter. Finally, she took the registration papers and plates off the truck, just to be on the safe side.

The bag had enough room to shove one of the blankets that James had grabbed into it. Jayden tied up the rest of the blankets with a rope and handed the bundle to Dreya. He used the rest of the rope to tie up the water jugs and he swung them over his shoulder. James secured the fly rod to his backpack and took the rifle from Jayden. He handed him the pistol which Jayden tucked into his waistband. They worked fast and then started walking.

"Let me take that," Mia said to Katrina easing the pack from her shoulders.

"I'm okay," Katrina said but Mia took it anyway.

From the top of the mountain they had a view of the entire valley floor below. To the right was a large town that they had avoided by taking the back road past the trailers. Everything was in miniature scale from this high up. Katrina could see no signs of life and no moving cars on the road. She sat down awkwardly on a rock. "Alright," she sighed. "Who has the needle?"

James pulled a sewing kit in an old tin cookie container from inside of his backpack. Dreya took it from him and sat down in the dirt next to Katrina's leg. He handed Dreya a bottle of rubbing alcohol and Katrina smiled.

"For the pain?" she winked.

"No dummy." He stared at her. "To clean the wound. Here's some ibuprofen for the pain." Katrina laughed and swallowed two pills. Then she clenched her teeth as Dreya washed the wound with the stinging alcohol. Dreya worked swiftly and sealed the wound up tight.

"Wow, that's really good," Katrina remarked as she checked out the stitches. "How'd you learn to do that?"

"Eh. You are still going to have a gnarly scar but it should hold up." Dreya stood and washed the needle before putting the sewing kit away. "I learned from my mom. Well, from her medical books. She is a surgeon."

Mia laughed. "All this time I thought you were such a nerd but look at it paying off now. Good job, Dreya." She smiled at her sister.

"Well I am glad we have a medical student in the group," James said. "Should we see what else we have now?"

"You got lucky today." Jayden unzipped the pack and pulled out a bag of Takis chips which he handed to Mia. "I remember you said that you missed these while we were in the shelter."

Mia jumped up and down hugging the bag to her chest. "Oh my gosh! Okay. I love you. Dreya, your boyfriend is seriously the best." Jayden flushed at the word boyfriend but Dreya gave him a warm smile.

James and Jayden emptied the rest of their packs onto the ground. Between the two of them, they had gathered cans of food, kitchen knives, a cooking pot, a box of salt, a bag of rice, Crisco grease in a can, plastic bowls, some electrical cords, a box of flies for the fishing rod, extra hooks and line, more rope, two flashlights, batteries, a box of matches, soap, a small first aid kit, bullets for the pistol, and an unopened box of Fruity Pebbles.

Katrina raised her eyebrows at the cereal box and James whistled as he turned away. They packed everything back up and started moving east into the wooded hills.

"You guys did good," Katrina laughed. "Hopefully we all get to share the Fruity Pebbles."

"Hey," Mia smiled back at her. "This isn't the society that we just ran from. If he doesn't want to share, then he doesn't have to." She held her Takis bag protectively.

"It's fine," James chuckled. "I don't mind sharing with anyone here. Those other guys were just jerks. No one wants to share with people like that."

Dreya put her arm around her little sister. "And you don't have to share your weird spicy roll up chips with anyone if you don't want to."

Mia stopped walking and held the open bag out. "Does anyone want some?"

"No thanks," they all laughed while walking past her. Mia smiled in triumph as she ran to catch up.

*

"It's going to get dark soon," James told Katrina as he helped her climb over a rock. She was sweating in her suit and her leg was throbbing.

"I know," she said. "I was just hoping that we could get further away from the road."

"I don't think that anyone followed us," James reassured her. "And you need to take a break."

Katrina was about to argue but she looked back to see Mia resting her arms on her thighs and breathing heavily after clearing the rock patch. Dreya nodded to Katrina after checking on her sister. "I guess this is as good a place as any to camp for the night."

"Guys," Jayden called out. "Look at your monitors." Katrina pulled hers up. The air was cleaner where they were standing. The device still showed being in a hot zone, but the numbers were dropping. Mia ripped off her mask.

"Hang on," Dreya shouted at her. "Wait until we talk about this."

Mia inhaled deeply as she smiled at her sister. "Oh come on in, the water is fine." Dreya slowly took off her mask and smiled back at her.

Jayden quickly took off his entire suit. "Screw hiking in that thing anymore. I think I'd prefer radiation tumors."

Dreya laughed. "I'm sure you'll get your wish someday."

"That's not funny," Jayden eyed her skeptically as she smiled at him.

"It's not funny," Mia laughed. "But we might as well make jokes about it. It's not like we can change anything. They dosed the earth in nuclear fallout, we just have to make the best of it." James looked to Katrina and she shrugged. They both removed their suits.

*

Katrina sat on the ground with her leg elevated on a rock while James built a fire. Jayden began to heat up some cans of soup over the flames in the stainless-steel pot they took from the house. They all shared the box of Fruity Pebbles for dessert. James scrubbed the pot with dirt and gravel before carefully rinsing it with a small bit of water.

Dreya checked out Katrina's leg. "You didn't break any stitches, so that's good," she said yawning.

"Let's go to bed," Katrina told her. "It will feel much better in the morning."

They laid close to one another wrapped in quilts from the trailer. James extinguished the fire and snuggled up against Katrina's side. She heard his snores and then turned to look up at the stars. Except there weren't any stars, just a blackened grey sky that stared back down at her. A tear escaped her eye and rolled down her temple into her hair as she bit her bottom lip. Katrina rolled back over to see James sleeping peacefully. She was too tired to think. She closed her eyes and slipped into a deep, dreamless sleep.

Chapter 6

The sun burned bright red through the morning haze. Katrina woke up to the sounds of someone vomiting in the bushes.

"Do you think the Takis were bad?" Dreya asked Jayden as she held her little sister's hair back.

Jayden read the bag. "They don't expire until next year and the package was sealed."

"It's probably a little altitude sickness," Katrina yawned and stretched out her arms. "We went from 6 ft underground to over 8,000ft in two days. She sat up and frowned at the sudden pain in her leg. Pulling her knee toward her, she started gently massaging her calf. "How do you feel now Mia?"

"Much better," Mia answered while wiping her mouth. "Still a little lightheaded but nothing like before. I was having trouble breathing and I think I ate too many Takis mixed with the cereal."

Katrina smiled sympathetically at her. "There is less gravity up here and it makes it harder to breathe. We can take it slow though. Unfortunately, the only cure is to go back down. People say the air is thinner the higher you go but really it's just your lungs working harder."

"Well I'm not going back that way," Mia laughed. "Let's keep going forward. I'll be fine."

Katrina nodded to her as she slowly stood up. "In a few days you'll relearn how to breathe. We will take it easy."

James started to make a fire for breakfast, but Katrina stopped him. "Why don't we share some MREs instead? It will be faster."

"Ugh. I'm going to throw up again," Mia gagged. "I don't know how much more of those my stomach can take."

"You can have the crackers," Katrina said winking at her.

*

They started off at an easy pace. Too slow for Katrina's liking but she was sore, and it was hard to even maintain that speed. When they crested the next hill, a valley dip lay stretched out before them that was thick with different types of pine trees dotted through with western juniper and quaking aspen. The tops of the trees were dusted with ash.

Katrina pointed to another mountain ridge in the distance. "That is where we are heading," she told her friends. "We still have a long way to go."

They climbed slowly down the mountainside and into the valley. Beneath the thick tree coverage, the ground was mostly free from the fallout. The pine needles crunched under their feet and a jack rabbit scurried away as they crashed through the underbrush.

"Did you see him?" James smiled to Katrina as he turned to point where the rabbit went. "He looks healthy. I told you they would be okay." Katrina returned his smile and they kept trudging through the brush. By midday they were exhausted, and Katrina was out of breath.

"Let's stop for a bit," Dreya suggested. Katrina was glad that she didn't have to ask.

They sat in the shade of a thick overhead tree canopy and shared a bottle of water. Buzzing filled Katrina's ears as she heard the insects of the forest move about. Out here it was getting easier for Katrina to distance herself from the events of the past few weeks. As they walked, she focused on taking each step carefully and tried to plan out the coming days in terms of food and water rations. Sitting there, the memories came in waves. Compartmentalize, she told herself. Take what you need and store the rest for later.

Her mind began to wonder. "Two weeks should be enough time for the air to clear," her dad had told her when he dropped her off that night at the fallout shelter. "This is the safest place for you… I need you to be safe so I can do what I have to do… If I'm not there when the doors open, get to the cabin." Katrina shouldn't have taken anyone with her.

She was taught that people were liabilities and how to do things on her own, but she liked these people. She had been forced to live in the shelter and she made friends. And James. James was kind of cute, Katrina smiled to herself.

They all had to run from the shelter after Lark and the rest of the kids tried to force them to stay in the society they were trying to build. The shelter could have been safe. It was run by an automated system, named Nanny, and would keep delivering food and clean water for a year. They could have stayed underground and waited to dig out. That's not important anymore, Katrina pulled back her thoughts.

Focus. What do I know about the surface so far? They blew up the planet and the sky is grey. Who blew it up and why? No answer to that. Some people had survived though, and they were scared. They didn't trust the government and they knew about this Project Dandelion thing. Project Dandelion. Nanny had said it was the government's attempt at repopulating the earth. Keeping a select group of kids alive after the world was blown apart. They had the dandelion gene and their parents had done something to better society so that's how they got their ticket in. Except James wasn't supposed to be there. His dad's girlfriend snuck him in.

Dang it, Katrina! Stop thinking about James already.

Okay. People survived. How did they know about the project? And why don't they trust the government? Probably because the government allowed this to happen. No, wait. Buzzcut had said he was going to use the kids as hostages to sell to the government. They are against the government now. Katrina put her head in her hands. The whole world was just a mess.

"Where are you?" James asked pulling Katrina out of her rabbit hole. He sat on the ground in a circle with Dreya, Mia, and Jayden. Katrina moved down from the fallen tree trunk she was leaning against to join them.

"Nowhere," she sighed. "Just wasting energy trying to figure this whole thing out."

Jayden laughed. "No use. We've all been trying to do the same thing. Did you think of anything that could help us though?"

Katrina shook her head. "Only that we need to stay far away from other people and get to the cabin."

"Agreed," they all responded.

"We should start hunting. We are going to need more food. And we need to think about finding some water, so we don't run out," James said while lifting Katrina's leg onto his lap. "If we find water, we might be able to find fish too."

"Nanny said the fish would be poisoned though." Dreya looked at him confused.

"Yeah, I know she said that." James scratched his head. "Hear me out. I have this theory that there might be pockets of water in some of the valleys up here in the mountains that aren't affected by the fallout. Those fish would be okay."

Katrina was looking at James. "That might actually be a good theory. Up over the next ridge there are several glaciers and small lakes that are fed from the snow melt and underground springs. We can check them out."

Jayden wrapped a blanket over his head.

"Are you cold?" Dreya asked.

"No," he said. "These bugs are driving me nuts."

"They aren't even that bad right now," Katrina said.

"How is a guy that shoots like you do afraid of a few bugs?" James laughed.

"I can't shoot bugs," Jayden shrugged. "You plan on actually using that rod to catch us some fish? It was hanging on the guy's wall. Who knows the last time it was used?"

"It's a good rod," James protested. "The line might be dry, but he had more right next to his box of flies. I grabbed it all." He leaned back against the rock. "You're just mad because you don't know the delicate art of fly fishing. Don't worry, I'll rig you up with a hook and a worm if that's all you can use."

"That's all talk right now man. We will see if you actually hook something first," Jayden said, and James smiled as he nodded at him.

Katrina was amused at their banter, but her leg was aching so she stood up to stretch.

"Are we leaving already?" Mia groaned. "I just barely sat down."

Katrina laughed. "We might as well get moving. If we are going to test out James' theory, we need to make it to about 10,000ft which is out of this valley and up those mountains."

"Ugh," Mia sighed as Dreya helped her up. "I don't even like fish that much.

Dreya laughed as she pushed her sister forward. "You're doing great love. Let's just keep going."

Chapter 7

It took three more days for them to cross the valley and make it up the side of the mountain ridge. Their pace was picking up as they adjusted to the altitude and Katrina's leg healed. James and Katrina showed the group how to construct lean-tos to sleep under each night. They laid branches and sticks at an angle against fallen trees or rocks to form a triangle hut. Then they weaved sticks or put grass and pine boughs across the top to make it more water resistant and warm inside.

"Like Nanny showed us on the documentary," Mia commented the first night. In the morning they scattered the makeshift shelters because Katrina didn't want to leave a trail to follow. By the third night, they were all experts at building the huts and had discovered ways to build them close to each other so that no one slept alone.

*

In the early morning of the third day, Katrina woke to a chill across her back. She reached behind her to find James' spot empty. Her heart skipped a beat as she sat up on her elbows to look for him. He probably just went to the bathroom, Katrina thought. She waited a few minutes but still couldn't hear him.

Crawling on her forearms, she carefully left their lean-to and stood barefoot on the dew soaked earth. How long had he been gone? She worried. She was sleeping so soundly since they had gotten to the mountains. There was no way she would have heard him when he left. Oh you big dummy, Katrina thought as she pulled her shoes on. She moved quietly so that she didn't wake the others.

She stepped away from the cluster of trees they had built their shelters beneath. The air was unnaturally still and the fog covering the dark sky only allowed a weak glow from the moon to pierce through. Katrina carefully climbed on top of a boulder to extend her viewpoint, but it was useless. She sat down and pulled her knees to her chest.

As the minutes passed, the fear that something happened to him kept edging on Katrina's thoughts. She pushed it away and steadied her breathing so that she could listen better to the sounds of the woods. What would I do if he didn't come back? she asked herself. Keep moving of course. Except, she knew that was a lie.

Katrina kept herself pressed against the hard rock so that she didn't go running around like an idiot in the dark. The moon was about to set. When the sun rose enough to give more light, she would wake the others to help her find him. Please don't let him be hurt, she thought.

The wind began to blow. A cool breeze chilled her through her thin t-shirt. She was glad they had chosen to blow up the world during summer. Winter would have made this suck even worse. She was just about to climb down from the rock to go get her blanket from the hut when she heard the distinct crunch of pine needles and rocks to her right. The sound grew louder as the footsteps came closer.

Katrina quietly slid down from her seat on the boulder and peered around the side until she saw James' face clear the trees. "What is wrong with you?" Katrina blurted out as she came from behind the rock.

James jumped. "What is wrong with me?" He put his free hand over his chest. "What is wrong with you? Why are you hiding behind a rock in the dark? You scared the crap out of me."

"I. Scared you?" Katrina's eyes widened. The grey hazy morning light had broken into the clearing where they were standing, and she saw he was holding the rifle at his side. "You weren't there when I woke up and you took my firearm. You scared me."

"A tough girl like you?" James winked. "Didn't think you got scared."

"I don't," she stammered. "Well, I did. Ugh. Just don't ever do that to me again." She couldn't stay mad while he was bouncing around and smiling at her.

"Don't do what?" He smiled ear to ear as he swung two dead rabbits from the rope on his shoulders and held them out to her. "Get you breakfast?"

*

"Bet you are glad I grabbed that can of enchilada sauce now," Jayden said laughing as he built the fire. Katrina and James each skinned one rabbit and cut the meat off in chunks.

"They don't look sick to me," James said. "But stay away from the meat near the bones just to be on the safe side." Jayden browned the meat over the fire and then let it simmer away in the pot with the sauce for an hour. He threw in some rice during the last 30 minutes.

Dreya winced as she took her first bite, but she quickly finished her bowl. "That was actually pretty good," she said to Jayden.

"That was better than good," Mia exclaimed. "That was bomb. Alright guys, I want to learn how to shoot. I need to get us some more rabbits."

Katrina smiled at her. "We'll teach you, I promise. Let's get over that mountain today though. It's going to be a rough hike and we will gain a lot of elevation, but James' hypothetical fish paradise is right over that ridge."

They cleaned the dishes and packed up their camp. The climb was steep, but they kept slowly moving up. Katrina's wound pain had eased, and she was left with only a dull ache. She had been careful not to break any stitches and had kept it clean, but it still needed more time to heal so she babied it as she climbed. The group came to a rocky part of the hillside with no way to go around it, so they went single file helping each other over the rocks.

Past the boulders, they were exposed on the side of the mountain with no tree coverage. It was getting harder to breathe and they began to walk even slower.

"Hey," Jayden smiled. "At least there are no bugs over here."

Katrina laughed as she pushed to keep moving forward. There was no comfortable place to sit and rest until they reached the top. They took sips of water, leaning against one another when needed, as they continued to inch up the hill.

It was late in the afternoon when James stepped first onto the plateau that stretched about five feet wide and topped the mountain side. The edge descended steeply into a bowled out small valley beneath their feet. He reached down his hand smiling as he helped Katrina, and then the rest of the group, up onto the slab to stand beside him. Everyone was out of breath and they sat down with their feet hanging over the ledge.

James spread out his arms. "Paradise," he said winking at Katrina. "We found it guys."

Katrina looked up to see that the sky seemed more bluish grey instead of the thick grey smog that she had been accustomed to seeing lately.

"It looks like we are higher than some of the clouds right now. Maybe the debris in the air is blocked by some of these mountains," Dreya said.

"Yeah but I am sure if it rains it will still be toxic or laced with fallout," Katrina shook her head.

They looked down at the valley below. It was small enough to cross in a few hours. To the right was a little pond with water that shimmered in the daylight and tiny streams fed into it before cutting ribbons through the earth down the smaller hills in the distance. The ridge that they sat on was a part of the mountain that enclosed the valley below them at the highest peak and protected the oasis like a fortress wall. Katrina raised her eyebrows as she looked back to James who sat there smiling at her.

"Okay. It's a potentially toxic paradise," he laughed. "But still a paradise."

The descent down the mountain was slippery as there were no trees or brush to grab on to. Mia sat on her butt and began to slide down instead of walking. The other kids laughed but quickly copied her.

"I think technically we just went sledding," Katrina said as they reached the bottom. "This is a glacier we are standing on."

Mia turned to look at the mountain. "Huh. I pictured a glacier looking a little less, I don't know, dirty?"

James took off running to the stream closest to where they were standing which rippled into the lake. He started lifting rocks and pulled Katrina over as she came near. "Look," he said. "Look at the nymph castings. The May flies are getting ready to hatch soon. It's the perfect time to fish." He dropped his pack and took off alone to check out the brooks.

Katrina and Dreya found a spot under some small pine trees to set up a camp.

"Think he will actually catch anything?" Jayden asked as he carried over a pile of sticks to start the fire.

"I think the question should be will he catch anything that we can actually eat," Katrina laughed. She went off to explore the hillside after they set up camp leaving Dreya and Jayden alone to sit and talk. Mia left to skip rocks on the water. Katrina walked along the base of the hill and thought of the years she had spent tagging along with her father as they hiked all over these mountains. He would tell her to watch the horizon and to pay attention to the ground in front of her. She used to think you'd have to be cross-eyed to do them both, but she had practiced so much she was good at it now. Always aware of your surroundings.

There were fresh tracks in the dirt, a marmot probably. She followed the tracks to its den and climbed slightly above the opening, careful not to disturb the entrance. Katrina found some sticks and rocks. Then she took the electrical cords and stripped off the plastic coating. Next, she braided the wires and created an improvised noose snare. She tied the end to a heavy rock on the left of the den entrance and gently held it up with a forked stick as a wire guide so it would lock around the marmot's body when it came through.

Once the snare was set, Katrina stood up and watched James fishing across the meadow. She followed the shape of his profile, starting with the outline of his jaw and remembered how it felt to kiss him the last night that they were in the shelter together. Warmth spread into her stomach and her heart quickened as she unconsciously touched her lips. Gosh he was cute.

James gracefully whipped the line of his fishing pole back and forth while he released more slack with his other hand. As he began gently tugging on the line to bring it closer, Katrina watched the line grow tight and he began furiously reeling it in. He dropped to his knees on the bank and then stood up directly facing her as if he knew exactly where she was. In his hand was a beautiful trout and a triumphant smile spread across his face. Katrina gave him a thumbs up. He quickly turned around to unhook the fish and get his line back in the water. She laughed as she made her way back to Dreya.

Jayden and Dreya were still lounging under the shade of the tree.

"He got one," Katrina called out as she walked up to them.

"We saw," Jayden called back. "Let's see if he can catch another though." Katrina sat down next to them. "What did you set a trap for?" Jayden asked.

"I think it's a marmot den over there. Guess we will just have to wait and see."

Dreya turned to look for her sister and her mouth dropped open. "Mia!" she yelled. "What in the world do you think you are doing?" Katrina and Jayden turned to look. Dreya put her hand over Jayden's eyes. "Put your clothes back on, right now!" Dreya screamed.

Katrina started laughing as Mia threw her shirt and pants onto the bank. She stuck her tongue out at her older sister and then dove under the water.

"Mia," Dreya called out as she ran to the lakeshore. "Get out of that water now. It's probably freaking toxic. This isn't some game."

Mia swam forward and then flipped to her back to kick water at her sister. "Come on Dreya. Don't be such a worry wart. We are probably going to die anyway, let's have some fun before we go." She gave her sister puppy dog eyes and Dreya turned around to look at Jayden and Katrina. Dreya shrugged and then stripped off her clothes before diving in. The two girls splashed around in the lake for a while. Jayden decided to join them.

"Come on Katrina," Dreya urged. "You stink. We all stink. At least get washed off."

"I don't want to get my stitches wet," Katrina called back from under the tree.

"It's been enough time, I think. The wound doesn't look open anymore. You can flush it out with rubbing alcohol when you get out." Dreya pushed out her bottom lip.

Katrina smiled as she walked over to the shore and carefully removed her clothes, folding them into a neat pile. She looked up to see James watching and gave him a wave before she sat down in the shallow water near the bank. Then she crossed her injured leg up over her other knee. "This is as deep as I go," she laughed.

Dreya swam over to her. "Here," she said climbing onto the bank, "turn around and let me help you rinse your hair. You can keep your leg out of the water." Dreya held the back of Katrina's head as she let her hair soak out into the water. Katrina's head felt weightless as the strands fanned out into the lake. Dreya massaged her scalp with her free hand and then ran her fingers through the knotted hair until it spread out smoothly in the water again.

"This feels glorious," Katrina sighed. "I'm pretending I'm at a spa."

"We should stay here a while," Dreya told her. "It feels safe. We should at least stay until your leg heals."

Katrina sat up and turned around. "We can stay a day or two, but we will run out of food if we stay much longer than that." Dreya stared at Katrina, her forehead wrinkled, then she nodded and swam away. Jayden grabbed Dreya by the waist when she returned and picked her up before dunking her back into the water. Mia's laughter echoed through the mountains. Katrina smiled as she watched them play. She ran her fingers through the sand under the cool water and then started to collect tiny colored pebbles to stack into a small mound.

Before long, James came walking up with a stringer full of trout. He laid the line in the water to keep the fish cold and then took off his t-shirt. Katrina watched his stomach muscles tighten when he lifted his arms. Her eyes traveled down to the lines of his hips and she quickly turned away blushing when he dropped his shirt to the ground.

"Enjoying the show?" He winked at her and her cheeks began to burn. "I stink like fish," he said smiling. "I'm going to go rinse off. I'll be right back." James glided through the water with each powerful stroke of his arms until he reached the others. Jayden put Dreya on his shoulders and Mia climbed up James' back. The sisters wrestled each other from their elevated seats. Dreya won by pulling Mia into the water first.

Katrina cheered them on from the shore. I'm glad I didn't leave alone, she thought. This would have been a sucky hike all by myself. James swam back to her and they sat on the bank as he told her all about the different types of trout he had caught and planned to catch. The day grew late and Mia finally agreed to get out of the water.

"You sure these are okay to eat?" Jayden asked as he salted the fish.

"Guess we will find out," James shrugged. "But they don't look sick, they look perfectly untouched."

Jayden fried the trout in a little oil for dinner and Katrina gathered Yampa roots to eat alongside the meat. At dusk, the boys went to look for worms so that Jayden could fish with James in the morning. Katrina went to check her trap and found a marmot in it. She skinned it and then cut off the meat which she put in a pot of salt water to soak.

"Does marmot meat taste any good?" Mia asked.

"Not really," Katrina laughed. "But I'll brine it overnight in the salt water to make it edible. I also found some wild onions growing over there so I can flavor it up." Mia grimaced but nodded her head.

At dark, they sat around the fire wrapped in blankets. Katrina leaned her head against James' shoulder and he unconsciously stroked the top of her head as he talked more about the fish. Katrina was almost asleep when she heard Dreya say, "I've been thinking about what happened at the town. How did they know about us and why did they call us Project Dandelion?"

"Well Nanny said we all have the dandelion gene. That's one of the reasons we were picked to live down there," Jayden answered her. "I'm assuming that is what the Project Dandelion is."

"Yeah, but his eyes got big when he figured it out and they were going to kill us because of it. The only reason they didn't is because he figured we were worth more alive." Dreya's brow furrowed.

Katrina cleared the sleep from her throat. "I've been thinking on it too. They were genuinely scared of the government for some reason and we were part of some government program, so they definitely didn't trust us."

"Did your dad tell you anything about this Project Dandelion thing?" Mia asked as she yawned.

"Not really. I know he was working on the survival lessons for it." James stopped touching her hair to watch Katrina's face. "He didn't tell me that or anything. I just know that he uses those same videos to teach the Marines and that was all a part of his program that we were learning." Katrina looked at James. "A few months ago, he did have a talk with me about radiation sickness, again."

"So, they've been preparing for this and setting up the shelters for a while then?" James asked.

Katrina nodded. "That's what I've been thinking."

"How do we even find out what actually is going on?" Dreya pulled her blanket tighter around her shoulders.

"Get to the cabin." Katrina closed her eyes again. "And hope my dad is there so that we can ask questions."

Chapter 8

The next morning Jayden and James went fishing as soon as the dawn broke through the sky. Katrina stayed wrapped up in her blanket as she started the fire. The kindling caught the flames from the dried grass and she carefully laid more branches on top. The smoke smelled bitter from the sap that hissed as it melted off the fresh wood. Once the fire was roaring, she went to pick wild onions. She rinsed the salt from the meat and then browned it in the pot along with the onion bulbs and some stinging nettle leaves that she carefully plucked from the stem. Then she added water and let it simmer. When Dreya and Mia woke up, she added the rice.

"This smells amazing," Dreya said as she blew on a spoonful of the stew. "Then again, after eating MREs for two weeks almost anything fresh smells good."

Mia looked skeptical but she took the bowl handed to her anyway. "Here goes nothing," she said taking a bite. Dreya and Katrina watched her intently as she chewed the meat. "That's actually not horrible," she said after swallowing. "But I prefer rabbit." Mia finished her bowl just as the guys returned.

"How's the marmot?" Jayden asked as he spooned out soup from the pot into his bowl.

"Better than I thought it would be," Mia laughed.

James put the stringer of fish in the brook next to their campsite and pulled out a spoon to eat his stew. "She can cook?" he said looking at Katrina. He blew on his spoon before taking a bite. "Mmm, she can cook."

Katrina smiled as she put her feet up. "Sure can, and you can do the dishes."

*

After the dishes were cleaned, Mia made the announcement that she wanted to learn how to shoot. Katrina pulled out the box of bullets for the pistol. There were twenty left. "We can't waste a bunch on shooting practice," she said. "But I think it will be okay to fire off a round or two."

Jayden went to put an empty soup can on a rock three yards away. Mia was shaking as she stood up to hold the gun. Dreya hung back and bit her bottom lip as she watched her little sister.

"This is important," Katrina told her. "The safety. This lever right here. This always stays on unless you intend to shoot. And by intend, I mean you better be ready to kill something." Mia nodded.

Jayden walked back up to them. "Don't scare the crap out of her Katrina." He smiled at Mia.

"It's serious though." Katrina narrowed her eyes. "Guns aren't toys. You have to know that you are holding a powerful tool in your hands and you should know how dangerous they can be before you choose to use that power."

"I agree," said Jayden, "but they are just tools. And if she keeps shaking like that, she'll never hit the target." Katrina sighed and walked back to stand by Dreya.

Jayden showed Mia how to hold the gun and breathe before she took the shot. They practiced dry firing and made sure she knew how to handle the weapon before loading the gun. He stepped back as Mia fired. The can went flying off the rock. Mia lowered the gun and pointed it at the ground like she was told to.

"Beginner's luck," James called out.

Mia rolled her eyes and Jayden walked out to set the can up again. He placed it at seven yards.

"Not a chance," James said as Jayden ran back. Mia took her stance and shot again. Clink. The can went flying. Katrina and James looked at each other wide-eyed.

Jayden gave them a big smile. "One more?" he asked Katrina. "Just to see?" Katrina nodded and Jayden ran out to fifteen yards. They all held their breath as Mia exhaled and fired off a final round. The can shot straight off the rock into the air. Dreya let out a loud whistle.

"Holy shit Mia," James said clapping her on the back. "You're a natural Annie Oakley."

Mia smiled as she clicked the safety back on and handed the gun to Jayden. "Nothing to it," she shrugged and walked away to go get the can.

*

After dinner, James took Katrina fishing. They walked to the far end of the valley to get to the stream he hadn't fished yet. Specks of bugs flew around them as dusk came closer.

"We haven't seen any birds," Katrina remarked as James got the pole rigged up.

"Did you think we would?" James asked as he finished tying on the fly.

"I guess not," Katrina said. "It's just so odd."

James showed Katrina how to stand and guide the pole so that the line danced between ten and two as she pulled out slack before letting the bug land delicately on the surface of the water. He was much better than she was, but she got the job done. She handed him back the pole and he hooked a trout on his first cast.

The golden skin on the fish's back glistened as the water beaded away and James held it out for her to see with a smile beaming across his face. The perfect photo, Katrina thought. Too bad she didn't have her phone. They took off their shoes and waded further down the shallow brook. The frigid water lapped at their ankles and Katrina laughed.

"What's so funny?" James asked grinning at her.

"Nothing," Katrina smiled. "Well nothing important."

"Come on," he nudged her. "You have that distant look again. I want to know where you are."

"Alright," she said. "When I was little, I went camping with my dad and we caught some fish for dinner. I caught the bigger fish and I was so proud of myself. Well as my dad was cleaning them in the stream, my fish slipped out of his fingers and floated away down the current. I walked barefoot through the freezing water for what seemed like an hour and I actually found the fish. It had gotten caught on a rock. I guess you could say that I caught that fish twice," she giggled. "I think that I was even prouder bringing it back the second time."

James stopped walking as he turned to face her. "You miss your dad a lot, don't you?"

"I do," she said. "But I hope he will be there at the cabin."

"And if he isn't?" James asked softly.

"Then I will wait. Or I'll go find him. I haven't gotten that far yet." Katrina watched as James quickly turned away from her. "What is it?" she asked him. "Are you thinking that you want to find your dad too? We can try if you want. Let's just go get the supplies from the cabin first."

James shook his head. "He would have been there when the doors to the shelter opened if he was still here. I've made my peace with that."

"And you think I haven't made mine…" Katrina's voice trailed off. "Oh. I get it. You think I am being stupid for not giving up hope." James reached out to grab her hand and she pulled it back. "You don't understand. He has been planning for something like this to happen all my life. If anyone would make it, it would be him. He told me he would be okay, and he doesn't lie to me." Katrina could feel her blood boiling and she didn't know why.

"He did leave the truck though, like he knew he might not be coming back." James shrugged.

"Yeah because we were supposed to meet at the cabin if he didn't show. He left it so I could get there." Katrina stormed out of the water.

"Wait," James called after her. "Don't get mad. I just want you to be prepared to face the possibility."

Katrina pulled her shoes onto her wet feet and glared at him as he crossed the rocks onto the shore. "You don't even…" James took Katrina's face into his hands and leaned down to kiss her.

She tried to pull back, but he wrapped his arms around her and hugged her tightly. She melted into him. Their lips met eagerly. Then James pulled his away- always too soon! Katrina screamed in her head- and he smiled sweetly at her.

"I'm sorry," he said. "Don't be mad. I'm just worried about you, probably more than I should be, and I don't want you to get hurt."

Katrina rolled her eyes. "Come on," she said. "It's getting late. Let's head back to the others."

*

"Alright. I'm getting tired of fish," Mia said picking the last of the meat from the bones as she finished breakfast. "I want to go find some rabbits today."

James laughed. "I'll take you to look for some in a little bit."

Katrina smiled at Mia's enthusiasm. "Hopefully you find some. We do need to get ready to start heading down the mountain tomorrow."

"What?" Mia crossed her arms. "Why do we need to leave so soon? Can't we stay here a little longer?"

"I'm sorry," Katrina shook her head. "We don't have supplies to stay here long term. This place is nice but at the rate James is going we will end up fishing out the whole valley soon. There isn't enough food here to sustain us. Plus, we need ammo, guns, and adequate shelter. All of that is at my cabin."

"Couldn't we just build a cabin here?" Mia grumbled.

"I'm sure we could," Katrina said, "but it would be a rough winter without supplies."

"Well, let's just get supplies then and bring them back here," Mia tried to reason. "Who knows what it is like over at your cabin anyway. We know the air is okay here and that the fish are good. The water hasn't killed us yet either."

"The cabin sits at just about the same elevation as this and that valley is just as nice, I promise you." Katrina sighed. "My dad chose that location on purpose."

"But I don't want to go."

"Mia," Dreya snapped at her sister. "Enough. We are going to the cabin. End of story." Mia looked to her feet and clenched her teeth.

"Come on kid." James put his arm around the girl. "Why don't we go look for your rabbits?"

*

They spent the afternoon filtering water to refill the jugs for their trip. Mia and James came back with three rabbits for dinner. Jayden made kabobs with the wild onions and rabbit meat. After dinner they boiled water to wash all the cookware and utensils. Dreya fixed her little sister's hair into tight braids but that did nothing to fix Mia's mood. She went to bed by herself as soon as the sun set.

Katrina picked the bark from a stick as they sat around the crackling fire. "How long is she going to be mad at me?" She asked throwing the stick into the flames.

"Not long," Dreya told her. "She is just scared, and it seems like we can finally breathe up here. Don't stress about it."

"We are all scared." Katrina pulled her knees to her chest. "The trick is to not make dumb decisions based on fear."

"But is it though?" Jayden leaned forward to join the conversation. "I mean, I'm down for whatever, but is it really that dumb of an idea to stay here? We do need to get supplies, but would it be that bad of a plan? We have been lucky so far with escaping those guys and not having anything major happen, but who knows how long that luck will hold out?"

Katrina sighed. "I guess it isn't an awful plan. We still would have to get supplies somehow and I am still going to the cabin. If it is better here than it is there, we can always come back."

"Good." James smiled at Katrina. "I like it here."

"And we are all going to the cabin with you," Dreya crossed her arms as she looked to Katrina. "We are all in this together."

Katrina smiled. "Do you think this will make Mia happier?" she asked.

"It makes me so freaking happy!" Mia yelled from inside her hut.

Chapter 9

The next morning, they rolled up their blankets to attach to their packs before scattering the camp and heading across the valley. When they crested the eastern most ridge, Mia turned to wave goodbye to their paradise before beginning their descent down the mountain. The next valley had a rocky climb down which led into the trees. They crunched their way through the fallen pine needles underneath the forest coverage. By dusk, the kids had climbed out of that valley and made camp on another ridge.

"Are we following the moss on the trees?" Mia asked. "Isn't that how you know which way is north?"

Katrina smiled. "The moss doesn't just grow on the north side of the tree. It grows wherever it is shady and damp. I'm following the sun and those mountains over there."

"They all look the same." Dreya raised her eyebrows. "What are the mountains telling you?"

"The snow pack on the mountains," Katrina laughed. "The snow melts faster on southern facing slopes so the heavier snow pack should be north."

"Are you sure you know where we are going?" Dreya asked.

"For the most part," Katrina answered.

*

A small river ran through the valley that they crossed the following day. The water was only calf deep, so they took off their shoes and waded across. Mia went first. When she reached the opposite bank, she let out a high-pitched scream. Dreya grabbed her little sister and turned her around to check if she was hurt. Mia extended her arm to point to the left and turned her head away from the sight. Dreya looked at where she was pointing and then ran to the bushes while gagging. Katrina and James rushed to the shore with Jayden trailing close behind.

A dead deer lay in the sand of the bank with his head propped up at an unnatural angle in the grass. It was bloated and flies were buzzing around the carcass. The stench made Katrina hold her breath.

"Did a coyote get it?" Katrina asked as James went to take a closer look.

He shook his head. "Look at the sores. It has no hair either. Radiation poisoning, I think."

Jayden quickly checked his monitor. "The air is still okay," he said. "How did that happen up here?"

"It didn't." Katrina turned away from the sight. "It happened somewhere else and she ran up to the mountains for safety."

Mia was shaking. "Is this what happened to mom and dad, Dreya? Is this what they look like now?" Dreya wiped her mouth and pulled her sister away to calm her down. Jayden walked over to help.

"That's what would have happened to me." James' voice was distant. "If Morgan hadn't snuck me into the shelter, my dad and I would have run up here." He turned to look at Katrina. "This is what happened to all of them, isn't it?"

She heard the pain in his voice and went to him. "Shh," she soothed. "We don't know that. He could be in someone's basement hiding right now for all we know." Katrina laid her palm on the side of his cheek.

James held her hand there. "That would be worse," he said. His eyes were crystal blue like the glacier fed streams. "If he stayed in a shelter he probably would have been shot by now." Katrina's face scrunched up in confusion. "Don't you get it?" he asked. "Those people in the trailer were shot point blank in their house. No one raided it, no one took anything, no one even cared what they had. It was someone who wanted them dead just because they survived."

"You don't know that…" Katrina's voice trailed away as she tried to piece together the situation.

"I do know that. I know that if my dad was alive, he would have been there when those doors opened. I know that I am here, and he isn't." Pain creased James' face in wrinkles by his mouth and nose.

"I'm sorry," Katrina whispered and kissed him gently on his lips. "I wish that I could take this away from you."

James rested his forehead against hers. "It's not your fault. Don't be sorry." He exhaled and stood up straighter as he tucked a lock of hair behind her ear. "I'm fine. Let's get going." The two of them linked hands as they walked over to their friends.

*

"Did I hear you say someone snuck you into the shelter?" Jayden asked James as they hiked up the hill.

"Oh yeah," James smiled. "I forgot to tell you all that. Technically I wasn't supposed to be there. My dad's girlfriend is in the Airforce and she got me in somehow."

Dreya stopped climbing as she turned to look at him. "How did she do that?" she asked.

"No clue," James said as he helped Mia over the rocky path. "It's not like parents tell us anything that is actually important." Dreya looked to Katrina and then back to James. "Is this a problem?" He smiled at her.

"Nope," Dreya resumed climbing. "It's surprisingly the least shocking thing that I've heard this month."

Chapter 10

At dinnertime they reached the top of the next mountain. A small village lay in the valley below them tucked between two lakes. There was one main road through the center and a handful of houses nestled into the mountain side.

"Well we are a lot closer than I thought we were," Katrina said as she peered at the valley below. "Over that next ridge line is a dirt road that leads to the cabin. We could probably make it by tomorrow night if we cut straight through but let's take the long way around to be on the safe side."

"I thought you said there were no more towns." Jayden sat down on a fallen log.

"I don't really consider this a town. It's more like an outpost where the guys who work at the ski resorts live and tourists come visit. The only business they have here is a little sandwich shop that I used to come to with my dad when we would fish the lake." Katrina sat down on the log next to him.

"I like the idea of going the long way," James said. "I don't want to take any chances again."

"It looks like there is no one there though." Dreya stood on a rock to get a better view.

"Oh!" Mia climbed up next to her sister. "Maybe we could get supplies and store them back up here. That way if we go back to our valley, we would have stuff we need and wouldn't have to carry it so far."

"That's a good idea," Jayden agreed.

"I don't think it is," James told him. "Remember we aren't trying to push our luck anymore?"

"But look," Mia said pulling James over to the rock. "There isn't anyone there. I think they all abandoned it."

James watched the town below. Nothing moved. "This feels like a bad plan," James said while climbing down from the boulder. "We should at least camp here tonight and keep an eye on it to make sure no one is really there."

"What do you think Katrina?" Mia asked coming over to sit next to her on the log.

"I don't know. I guess we could use some extra food, but it is a risk." She looked over to James. "I'm willing to do whatever you guys want though." Mia jumped up and hugged Katrina so hard they almost fell off the log.

"Keep your voice down Mia," Jayden laughed. "We are on a stakeout."

James walked away from the group and sat on a bed of pine needles as he leaned his back against a thick tree trunk. Katrina wiggled herself out of Mia's arms and left the others to set up camp as she went to sit with James. She slid down onto the ground beside him and picked up his hand to hold. "You alright?" she asked him.

"Mmm," he mumbled.

"If you are upset you can tell me."

"It's just a dumb idea."

"It isn't that bad of a plan. Besides it looks like it is a ghost town down there."

"It probably is," James smirked. "They are more than likely all dead."

"I'll go in so that you don't have to see anything." Katrina traced the fingers of her free hand down his forearm.

"It isn't that. I can handle that. It's just a risk that we don't have to take, so why take it?" James turned to face her.

"It's a diplomatic decision." Katrina gave him a defeated smile. "Majority rule."

"Well if you are the leader then you get to veto that rule."

"I'm not the leader," she laughed. "I was going to do this alone remember? But now we are doing it as a group. What kind of leader would I even be? I've got my own agenda and I'm selfish."

James smiled at her. "I'd follow you."

Katrina sighed. "I'd follow you too." He leaned over and kissed her softly on her forehead. She scooted closer and laid her head on his shoulder. "I don't think he is dead," she whispered. "My dad. I think he is okay somewhere. He couldn't have left the truck for me if he wasn't."

"Okay," James said as he smoothed down the top of her hair.

"But just so you don't think I'm delusional. If he didn't make it, well my plan is to honor his life by surviving and living the rest of mine. I don't know much but I do know that life is precious and worth fighting for." Katrina nodded her head and put her chin up in the air.

"Okay," James laughed as he wrapped her in his arms for a crushing hug.

*

They shared another MRE with two cold cans of beans for dinner that night because they didn't want to risk giving themselves away by the light of the fire. Jayden climbed higher into the rocks to watch the town.

"Anything happen yet?" James called up to him as they were getting ready for bed.

"Nah, man. Not even a mouse moving down there," Jayden yawned.

"I'll take a shift," James said as he began to climb the rocks. "Get some sleep."

Katrina watched as James settled into his guard position. Then she cuddled under the quilt and tucked it all around her. The night was dark, but the distorted light from the moon reflected off the boulders giving them an eerie glow. They would make tomorrow quick, she thought. In and out, then on their way. They could use the extra supplies.

She and her dad had been stocking the cabin with canned and dehydrated foods for years. Every trip they made up there they brought more. There was medicine and water, even a good water filtration system- better than the dirt filter they had been using. Guns and ammo, seeds and tools, traps and fishing gear. Plus, a CB radio. She had even left a few books and board games there for rainy days. They were prepared for the two of them. A few extra kids wouldn't hurt the stock pile that much but having more wouldn't hurt.

All the times her dad had drilled the doomsday stuff into her head. She mentally cursed herself for secretly doubting him. He had been planning for the worst-case scenario and that day had come. He was right and right now the cabin sounded like her idea of paradise. She remembered her dad standing in the creek gold panning as he talked to her about life, told her to be ready for anything. The fresh mountain air and the water bubbling clear down the valley full of wildflowers and spring. Katrina rolled to her side to try and get a rock out from underneath her back. Two days, she smiled to herself as she drifted to sleep. Two days and we will be there.

*

"I didn't see anything move all night," James whispered as he climbed under the blanket next to Katrina.

"What time is it?" she asked sleepily as she curled up next to him.

"Before dawn." He pulled her body against his and wrapped his arms around her. "I'm going to close my eyes for an hour or two."

"Uh-huh," Katrina muttered as she fell back asleep in his embrace.

Chapter 11

The morning sun was a brighter red-orange than it had been since they left the shelter. Jayden was sitting perched on the boulders overlooking the town when Katrina peeked out from under the blanket.

"Anything?" James called out still holding Katrina next to him.

"Not a single movement," Jayden said as he climbed down the rocks.

"Let's go then," Mia said bouncing around. They ate a quick breakfast, packed up, and headed into the village.

"Stay together," James warned as they neared the main street. "We hit one house and then we get out of here as fast as we can."

They crossed the road to a blue house with a red painted door. A white wooden rocker sat on the front porch surrounded by windchimes. A brown faded welcome mat lay on the doorstep dusted with ash.

"Mia, you are going to stay out here," James said looking to Dreya. She nodded and stood on the porch with her little sister. Jayden handed Mia the pistol.

The inside of the house looked like no one had been there in years. There was dust accumulated in every corner and cobwebs along the ceiling trim. Mixed plaid patterns lined the curtains, pillows, and furniture. "Gone Fishing" signs hung along the hallway.

"It might be a vacation rental," Katrina remarked as they walked into the living room. "I'll go check if they have any food."

"At least we won't find any bodies," Jayden said as he headed upstairs. He rummaged through the hallway closet. "Score!" he yelled down to his friends. "Sleeping bags."

Katrina laughed as she walked into the kitchen. She began to open the cabinet doors to find dozens of mismatched coffee cups and plates. In the cabinet by the refrigerator there were a few cans of chicken broth hidden behind an old spice rack. She took them along with a half open bag of coffee, plus the sugar and garlic powder. On impulse, she opened the refrigerator door and was greeted with the pungent stale smell of mildew coming from the empty shelves. "This place isn't really stocked for people to live," she called back over her shoulder as she put a kitchen knife into her bag.

James came into the living room with a hammer, nails, and a spool of wire he had found. Jayden tossed the sleeping bags down the stairs.

"Guys, hurry!" Mia shouted from the front porch. "Someone is coming!" James turned to Katrina with his eyes blazing icy blue. He took the rifle from his shoulder sling and ran out the door. Katrina scanned the room quickly and grabbed the cast iron fire poker next to the wood stove as she rushed to join her friends. She opened the door to see Mia pointing the pistol down the road.

"Put your guns down," a man's voice called from the street. Katrina turned to see three men walking up all carrying rifles.

"Maybe you should put your guns down first," Dreya called back in a voice so calm that it almost made Katrina laugh.

"Keep your gun up," James whispered to Mia. Jayden opened the screen door and came out from behind Katrina to stand in front of Dreya just as she called out again.

"You guys can put your guns down. We aren't looking for a fight. We are leaving and we will leave the stuff here if you want."

The man in the wide brimmed brown leather hat with a pink button up shirt and cargo shorts grinned. "We know you aren't looking for a fight and you can take whatever you need from there." He turned to the other two men and all three laid their guns down in the street. "Come on out and talk."

Dreya looked to Katrina and raised her eyebrows. "Do you know who we are?"

The man in the hat rubbed his chin. "Well, let's see. You aren't infected with radiation poisoning and you are just a bunch of kids, so I'd say you are either unnaturally lucky survivors or you all are Project Dandelion. Go ahead and put the guns down now. I don't feel like getting shot today." Dreya put her hand on Mia's shoulder and she lowered the pistol.

James looked over to her but kept the rifle pointed. He shook his head. "I'm not trusting them."

"I'm not asking for you to trust us boy," the man in the hat said. "I'm just asking for you to not shoot us."

"And why wouldn't I?" James turned to face the man. "What do you want with us?"

"Want with you?" The man laughed. "We've been watching you up on the hill since last night, hoping you would leave us alone. But now we can see that you are scared and in need, so we figured we would help. Put the gun down son, let's just talk. I can get you kids a decent meal."

Dreya smiled. "I think this one is okay James." He shook his head again.

Dreya nodded to her sister and then stepped out from behind Jayden to walk down the steps into the street. Mia followed her while James, Jayden, and Katrina stayed under the porch. She walked up to the man and extended her hand to shake his. "What's your name?" she asked.

"Tom," he smiled at her. "What's yours?"

"Dreya and this is my sister, Mia. Forgive my friends but we are all a little on edge. The only other people we met on the surface tried to take us as hostages to sell to the government. My friends aren't in the mood to trust anyone else right now."

"I see," Tom nodded his head. "And where are these other people at?"

"Down in the valley below where the mountains started."

"Lowlanders," the man to the right of Tom spit on the ground. "Idiots think they can trust the government now?" Dreya turned to look at the man who spit. He put his hands into the pockets of his faded Levi jeans and shrugged at her.

"Forgive my friend," Tom said smiling. "He is a little rough around the edges and he never really did trust the government. Guess we all should have listened to him."

"Speaking of that," the third man with the grey dreadlocks and tie-dye t-shirt interrupted, "I'm on edge myself standing out here in the open man. I think we should go." He looked up to the sky.

"Ziggy is right," Tom agreed. "Why don't you kids come back with me and my wife will fix you up some lunch." He held out his arm.

Dreya held her sister's hand and looked back toward her friends. James shook his head still holding the rifle as Jayden stepped down from the porch.

"I trust him," Dreya said to Katrina. "I want to ask some questions." Katrina nodded and put her hand on James' shoulder.

He sighed and lowered the rifle as they went to join them. "This is stupid," he whispered and Dreya gave him a big smile.

*

Down the street, the Levi man left the group and went into an old log cabin sitting on the hill.

"Where is he going?" Jayden asked.

"Home," Tom laughed. "We just met up this morning to go talk to you kids. Now he has to get back to work."

Tom and Ziggy led them into a cape cod style house with white shutters and a sloping roof. The interior of the house was covered in knickknacks and china cabinets displayed various painted tea cups. A grand piano sat against the sitting room parlor wall. Katrina looked around in confusion.

"This isn't mine," Tom said. "Or I guess it wasn't mine. It was the widow Farley's. She went on vacation last month. I figure she isn't coming back now. This is one of the only houses up here with a cellar."

They walked down a dark set of stairs leading away from the kitchen. The smell of earth filled Katrina's nose before they even stepped foot onto the dirt floor. Her heart began to pound as she remembered being trapped in the shelter and digging their way out.

The room was damp and musty. Two small oil lanterns lit the center of the room. Large seating pillows were strewn about the floor. Chinese room dividers sectioned off the three corners. Against the wall were shelves of food with a makeshift kitchen in the middle of them. Ziggy laid down on one of the floor pillows.

A slender woman in a long skirt with glasses sliding down the bridge of her nose came out from behind the divider in the far corner. She smiled lovingly at Tom as he hugged her.

"This is my wife, Sophie," he said to the kids.

"You all must be starving," she said softly. "I'll fix you something to eat. I just got the baby to sleep though so if we can try and be quiet, I'd really appreciate it." Ziggy rolled over and put his fingers to his lips as he shushed the kids. "Not that quiet,"

Sophie rolled her eyes. "Go sit down and make yourselves at home."

Dreya and Mia walked over to the cushions to sit down. Katrina and Jayden slowly followed. James leaned back against the wall.

"You can come sit down," Mia said to him. "They aren't going to feed us before they kill us." James didn't move.

"It's okay," Tom said as he sat down. "Let him stay where he is comfortable." Tom winked at him. James stared straight ahead.

Katrina sat cross legged on her pillow. "Thanks for inviting us in but I don't know why you would do it." She was nervous and uncomfortable, but she kept her voice steady.

"She means to say thank you." Dreya glared at her. "You have a lovely home." Ziggy, Tom, and Sophie all laughed.

"She's right though," Tom said after he caught his breath. "Except after what we've already seen, you kids are a sight for sore eyes. What did the president call them Zig? The hope for humanity or something like that?"

"Us?" Jayden asked. "How does the president know us?"

"Well not you five specifically but the whole Project Dandelion thing." Tom smiled at him. "I think it was supposed to make the rest of us feel better, that humanity would live on even though the world was being blown to pieces. The television broadcast from the president right before the power went out was a tearful farewell. He said they had top secret locations around the country with teenagers hidden safely away to ensure the survival of our species."

"But they sure didn't care about the other species on earth, did they now Tom?" Sophie called over from the kitchen area. She shook her head as she started the battery powered ceramic camp stove.

"We knew that," Dreya nodded. "At least that is what Nanny told us in the shelter." She looked back to Sophie. "Nanny was the electronic system recording telling us what to do," she explained. "But we don't know what happened after we got there, the night the bombs went off. Can you tell us exactly what it is you've seen so far?"

Tom looked to his wife. She wiped her hands on her skirt and nodded to him encouragingly. He ran his hand over his face. "Ziggy and I were drinking some beers that night watching the game. The broadcast came on towards the end. We never got to see the final inning. Sophie was upstairs putting the baby to bed. It lasted maybe five minutes. The president had sweat rolling down his chin. He said nuclear weapons had been fired and that more were coming. It was basically a hopeless apology with the dandelion kid thing thrown in there as a buffer. The broadcast cut out when the power went out. We thought for a minute that we wouldn't experience anything way up here. We tried calling friends that lived far away but there was no signal. We couldn't even get online."

He massaged his temples with his fingertips. "Ziggy was the one who saw the clouds coming over the horizon. This crazy guy climbed up on our roof to take a look. We grabbed Claire, our baby Claire, from the crib and we broke into Mrs. Farley's house to stay down here. I remembered she had a cellar because she asked me to carry some boxes down last year for her. We stayed down here almost a week before we went outside. Claire hasn't even been outside since then. Sophie takes her upstairs to sit by the windows a few times a day so that she can get some sun." Tom leaned forward and draped his long arms over his knees.

"About five days?" he asked Ziggy who nodded in response. "It was about five days later when the first of the people came up here. Those first ones were the worst. Their skin was falling off their bones and they vomited all over the street the minute they got out of the car. The old lady was gone before she stood up straight. Her son kept trying to save her with his blistered hands. He died a few minutes later. We had a break for a few days and then a whole bunch of them came. Spread out over about a week. These ones weren't as sick looking, but they still had radiation poisoning. The shakes and bruises and weakness. They started telling us stories about government check points on the roads and the military shooting whoever came through. None of them made it for more than a few hours, except Lacy. She lasted two days. We've buried twenty people on the other side of the lake so far. No one has come by the past couple of days except you all though."

Mia looked pale. Katrina bit her lip as she turned her face to the ground. Government, military, shooting unarmed civilians? Her mind raced and her stomach was in a knot.

"Why?" Dreya asked with tears in her eyes. "Why aren't they helping them?"

Chapter 12

"Don't you understand girl?" Ziggy asked from under his arm, still laying on the pillow on the floor. "It's mass exodus. Global cleansing. They are literally killing off the population so they can build their new world."

Mia shook her head. "I don't understand."

"Haven't you been paying attention?" Ziggy suddenly sat up. "They've been trying to silence us for years. We keep hearing about overpopulation, starving kids no one seems to care about, terrorists, globalization going sour because no one wants to adhere to the rules that the U.N. or I.M.F. keeps shoving down their throats. They took it a step further, well like off the deep end further, and decided to downsize the population into a more manageable size."

Ziggy put his hands behind his head. "Now they can have their new world order controlled by a single government. They've been testing this plan for years, right under your noses. You think Chernobyl or Fukushima or Three Mile Island in Pennsylvania were just accidents? They've been studying how to best survive and what would happen to the earth during a nuclear disaster for a long time."

"Do you believe this guy?" Jayden asked Tom with his eyebrows raised.

"I didn't," Tom sighed, "but now I wish I had believed him sooner. One of the guys who came up here said he talked to his mother in South Korea during the broadcast and their president was saying the same thing, like identical to what we were hearing. Almost as if the same message was sent to everyone to read. A woman whose husband was on a business trip in Sweden heard it too. "Maskrosbarn" is what they said, the dandelion child will carry on."

"But why us?" Dreya's forehead was creased. "I know we have the dandelion gene or whatever but what makes us so important?"

Ziggy laughed. Tom shook his head and gave her a sympathetic smile. "You'll have to ask him," he said pointing to Ziggy. "He's the psychologist."

"That guy?" Mia asked in disbelief.

Tom laughed. "Don't let his dirty hippie hair fool you. Ziggy studied at Colby College and was a top psychologist at John Hopkins Hospital for nearly twenty years."

"That was a lifetime ago." Ziggy turned to stare at Dreya. "Nothing is important about you, that's just the point."

Sophie came over carrying lunch on a tray. "The bread's a little stale, sorry. I've been trying to bake fresh loaves daily in my cast iron Dutch oven over the fire. Except we weren't allowed to have fires last night or this morning because the scouts didn't want us to advertise that we were here to you guys." She carried a plate with bread, dried salami, and a cup of tomato soup over to James.

"Why?" he asked her.

"We didn't know what you wanted until we saw you trying to get supplies from the rental down Main Street." Sophie smiled at James and he nodded his head before digging into the food.

Katrina's ears grew hot. They had been watching them. How did she not see that? Probably because she was too busy cuddling up next to James. She quickly shook the feeling of embarrassment away. They'd be more careful next time. She spread grainy mustard onto the bread and wrapped the salami up in it. The sandwich tasted like heaven.

"If we aren't important then why go through all this trouble to save us?" Dreya brought the conversation back.

Ziggy wiped away the breadcrumbs from the whiskers on his chin. "It's the gene. They are saving you because the gene isn't important. At least not in the traditional meaning of the word. This was all just a theory back when I was working at the hospital, but they've made great leaps in the research since. The gene that is the important one is the orchid gene.

CHRM2 is what they called it. This is the gene that makes the artists, the intellectuals, the great leaders, the ones who feel things as long as they receive the right environment to grow up in. They need love and nurture in their childhood. If they don't get treated well, then you get your criminals, your addicts, and your trouble makers."

Katrina stared at the old man as he continued. "Then you have your dandelion kids. Which is the opposite gene from the orchid one. These are the people with the genetic makeup that allows them to survive anything no matter the environment. No amount of suffering truly affects them. They can adapt to any situation. They don't cause trouble and don't do anything all that remarkable. They just are. The government wants only these types to survive in their new world. They want to breed out the ones that will change it."

Dreya's eyes went wide and Katrina smirked. "They don't seem to know us that well. Apparently, trouble is all we cause."

"I wouldn't advertise that if I were you." Ziggy looked straight at her with his piercing eyes.

"How do they know what genes we have?" James asked from the back of the room.

"Are you kidding?" Ziggy responded. "They've been testing you and recording you since birth. Right up there with your APGAR scores and your first prick with a needle for a blood draw. Your DNA is whisked away and analyzed in a government research center. They store it in the system so they can keep records of every citizen. Why do you think homebirths are considered so dangerous now? We've been born at home since the beginning of humanity but now they want to document your first breath so they can keep tabs on you."

Mia rolled her eyes. "Doesn't conspiracy theorist fall somewhere in the spectrum of mental disorders?"

"Little girl," Ziggy sighed as he laid back on his pillow. "Can you honestly look outside today and think anything could be more shocking? Believe it or don't believe it. This is your reality now."

The door to the stairwell leading down to the cellar opened. A teenage boy who had long hair to his shoulders and was wearing a black Nirvana t-shirt came running down the stairs yelling "dad!" He stopped at the bottom step when he almost ran into James.

"Right here Tripp," Tom said standing up. Tripp paused before stepping around James and entering the room. "It's okay," Tom reassured him. "These are our guests. What's going on?"

Tripp scanned the room. "There were tanks on the road heading up this way. I ran back as fast as I could."

"Did you tell Jones' family?"

"Margret saw the trucks. I met her at the creek as she was running home. She said she'd warn the Elisas too," Tripp blurted out breathlessly.

"It's alright. You did a good job son. Go catch your breath," Tom said.

"Come here and get something to eat Tripp," Sophie told him as she fixed a plate of food. He sat down on a pillow and Mia extended her arm gracefully.

"Hi. I'm Mia," she said in a low voice laced with honey. Dreya nudged her sister's leg. "What?" Mia asked. "I'm just being polite." She gave Tripp an adoring smile.

"No," Dreya said. "You're being uncomfortably awkward."

"Well it wasn't awkward until you said that." Mia ran her fingers through her hair, tilting her head to the side. "That's my much older sister," she whispered to Tripp. He blushed as he took a bite of his sandwich. Ziggy and Tom walked upstairs to check out the street.

"We need to go," James said as they left.

"Agreed." Jayden and Katrina stood up.

Dreya bit her lip and then pulled Mia to her feet. "Thank you so much for your hospitality and I hate to eat and run, but we should probably get going now," she told Sophie.

"Nonsense," Sophie said. "You stay here where it is safe." The baby began to cry, and Sophie ran to get her. They heard the vibrations of the treads on the asphalt as the trucks pulled onto Main Street above them just as Tom and Ziggy came running down the stairs. Tom bolted the door and Ziggy ran to the chest at the far wall. He pulled out rifles and ammunition from the crate while Sophie shushed Claire. Ziggy passed the guns around the room.

James walked to Katrina. "We need to get out of here. This is suicide," he whispered in her ear.

Katrina's brain kicked into hyper focus. They were trapped underground with no escape route. They could try and shoot whoever came through the door, she thought. But who knows how many were out there? Plus, what if they didn't come through the door? What if they just burned them out? It'd be safer trying to run. They should never have come down here. She shouldn't have listened to Dreya. They kept making too many mistakes. Ugh- think of a plan, Katrina screamed inside her head.

There wasn't time for a plan. A man on a loudspeaker from one of the trucks spoke, "Come out now. We know you are hiding here and I'm not playing any games today. The drone flying overhead saw five of you in the street earlier. I want all five people outside in the street immediately. Otherwise

I'm burning this place to the ground. You have until the count of ten. One."

Tom looked at the kids and then back to his own son and daughter. "I think it might be time for you guys to get going," he said to Dreya.

"Two."

"Tom. Stop it! They are just children." Sophie's chin trembled as her eyes welled with tears.

"Three."

The baby whined and Sophie rocked her.

"Four."

James walked to the stairs and lifted his rifle. Katrina grabbed a .22 from Ziggy.

"Five."

"It's okay," Dreya said looking at baby Claire. "You've been so kind, and we don't want her to get hurt."

"Six."

Dreya grabbed Mia and they rushed over to the steps.

"Seven."

Ziggy yelled, "Go through the dining room on the right. The sliding door leads out back away from the street."

"Eight."

They unlatched the cellar door and went running through the house past the table and through the glass door that James threw open.

"Nine."

Katrina heard another man call out, "Sarge! They are running through the trees."

"Open fire."

A bullet whizzed past Katrina's head as she took off running. The next few moments were like a dream. Her focus slipped into tunnel vision as she saw the bullet fly into the bark of the tree beside her causing it to splinter into flying fragments of wood. She kept running.

James was up ahead of her to the left. She watched him slip behind a growth of skinny aspen as he made his way forward. They were about to pass the last house in the village when she heard Mia's blood curdling scream. Katrina jumped behind a large pine tree trunk and James locked eyes with her briefly before she peered around the tree to look at the street.

There were men in solid green jumpers pulling Mia onto the main road by her hair. Mia's right arm was dangling as blood came pouring from it. She was kicking out at the men as they dragged her.

"It's a kid, Sarge!" one of the men yelled.

"I don't care who it is. Get the others."

Jayden came running out into the open and tackled the man who was hanging onto Mia's hair. Dreya ran and jumped on top of her little sister, using her body to shield the blows from the men who came over swinging batons. They grabbed Jayden and smacked the baton across his back. He buckled to his knees. Another man kicked Dreya in the ribs and Katrina heard her cry out, but she didn't move away from protecting Mia.

Katrina looked back to James. He shook his head "no". She took a deep breath in and watched the worry crease his face. "I have to. I'm sorry," she whispered as she left the cover of the trees.

Katrina ran out onto the main street holding the .22. There were three Humvees, she counted, and a tank in the rear. The sergeant stood on the tank. She aimed for him as she ran toward her friends. From behind her, she heard James yell, "damn it!"

Just before she pulled the trigger, a man she didn't see took the butt of his rifle and smashed it into the side of her head. She crumpled to the pavement.

Pushing up to her hands, she was kicked by the man so hard that she turned on to her back. Through the ringing in her ears she heard Dreya call out, "Stop! Please. We are Project Dandelion."

It didn't work fast enough to stop the man from kicking Katrina again. She saw James dive over her as he lunged to wrestle the man away. Then she rolled her head to the side and traced the outline of the mountain ridge to the east with her eyes. It's just over that peak, she thought as the darkness clouded her vision. I almost made it Dad.

Chapter 13

Katrina awoke in the back of the Humvee with Dreya roughly rubbing her knuckle into Katrina's chest bone.

"Stop that," she groaned as she rolled to her side. James was sitting next to her head on the floor of the truck with his knees pulled up to his chest. "I'm sorry," she whispered looking at his face.

"Mmm-hmm," he grumbled as he looked outside. Katrina sat up and her head screamed out in pain as bright flashes of light blinded her eyes. James saw her wobble and scooted closer to help hold her upright. The engine started and Katrina whipped her head around- which she instantly regretted- to see Jayden and Mia sitting up on the bench seat to the right. Mia had a bandage wrapped around her forearm and her teeth were chattering but she looked okay.

Katrina looked to Dreya. "Tom?" she whispered. Dreya shook her head and smiled as the trucks roared to life. They turned the vehicles around and headed down the mountain.

*

The teens shifted around in the Humvee as they made their way across the winding mountain roads and came back to the highway. One truck was behind them followed by the tank in the rear.

"Where are they taking us?" Dreya asked Katrina.

"I don't know," she said. "Your guess is as good as mine."

"I hope not. Isn't your dad in the military? If these guys are still around, couldn't your dad be too? Maybe they can take us to him." Dreya was busy trying to work out a plan.

"Honestly," Katrina broke the news to her. "I don't even know what to think anymore. When I saw these Humvees on the road, I should have felt relief. I've been around trucks like these and men like that my whole life. Except I was terrified of them. I don't know who these people are. I don't even know what uniforms they are wearing. What did they say to you when we got loaded up?"

Dreya's eyes filled with tears and Katrina saw the hope fade from them as she quickly blinked them dry again. "Nothing really. After I told them we were Project Dandelion everyone started cussing a lot. The guy on the tank used the radio and said he was bringing us in. Then they wrapped up Mia's arm as James carried you over. They put us back here and I woke you up."

Katrina nodded. "Okay. They might be in trouble for hurting us. That's good to know. I think we will be safe for a while. It looks like we are headed further east. I guess it's time to come up with a new plan."

"We should have listened to James and not gone into that place," Mia said through clenched teeth. "I'm done making plans. Whatever you guys decide, I'm in. But if it includes a doctor or a hospital, I'd appreciate it."

"We will get you taken care of," James said still staring out the back at the mountains. "First, let's just find out what is coming next." Katrina nodded and then leaned her throbbing head against James' shoulder. She closed her eyes so that she wouldn't see the mountains as the trucks drove away from them.

*

The facility they drove up to was encased in barbwire fencing with stakes set four feet high. A group of soldiers came running out to open the fence laid across the entrance for the approaching trucks. They all wore gas masks and Katrina felt naked without hers. From inside the central building, people came out with wool blankets which they wrapped around the kids as they led them inside as a group. They were walked single file through a dark hallway and led to two separate locker rooms.

"Don't split us up," Jayden yelled as he resisted being pushed into the men's room.

"It will just be for a moment," the woman with the sharp nose and tight bun high on her head said as she took Mia into the women's room. "We need to get you all cleaned off."

In the women's locker room sat two long rows of metal benches surrounded by open shower stalls. "We need you to undress and shower," the woman with the bun said. "Don't worry about your clothes. We will get you some new ones."

"What is this place?" Katrina asked as she slipped her shoes off.

"It's a holding facility," the woman said as she started to unwrap Mia's bandage.

Mia winced and Dreya stepped over. "I can do that," she said.

"Who are you holding if you are just shooting everyone?" Katrina pulled her t-shirt up over her head.

"It wasn't supposed to be like this." The woman's voice was flat.

Mia cried as the shower water hit her arm. The woman rushed over to her. "It's okay sweetheart," she said. "Just rinse it off really good and we will get you into medical to fix that up after."

Katrina turned on the water and it instantly became hot. She let the spray pelt down her back as she rested her forehead against the cool cement wall. The water massaged the bruises on her ribs where the man had kicked her.

Too soon, more people came in with towels and clothes. Katrina dried her hair and put on a pair of green sweats that were handed to her. Then they were shuffled out of the locker room and into a conference room that held a big table surrounded by cheap leather rolling chairs.

"We are going to take her to the medical bay," the woman said directing Mia away from the room.

Dreya spun around. "She is my little sister. She doesn't go anywhere without me." The woman paused.

"Katrina needs to be seen too. One of your thugs knocked a gun into her head," James said. "Actually, you know what? We are all going together." He walked towards the door.

The woman looked at the kids with panic in her eyes. "How about I bring the doctor here? You all just have a seat."

*

After the doctor stitched Mia's arm and checked out Katrina's head, five Styrofoam trays with macaroni and meatloaf were brought in for them to eat. Each tray also had an apple on it. Chewing the apple hurt Katrina's face, but every crisp bite felt amazing on her tongue and soothed her throat with the sweet juice. An elderly man came to clear the trash and the kids were left alone to wait.

James was pacing by the window and Katrina almost fell asleep in the chair when the doors swung open. In walked the sergeant from the tank earlier. Behind him came a tall man in military fatigues with brown hair shaved close to his head in a high and tight. Her heart started pounding and she sat straight up in the chair but when he entered the room, she realized it wasn't her father. Katrina leaned back in the chair and rubbed her forehead.

"Want to explain to me what the hell you were doing up in the mountains?" The big man said as he came to the table.

Katrina smirked. "We felt like going camping."

"You think this is funny, little girl?" the man screamed at her. She started to giggle uncontrollably. Her friends turned to look at her with their jaws slack which made Katrina laugh harder.

"How about a little more respect for Colonel Adams?" the sergeant snapped.

Katrina stopped laughing and stared at him with cold eyes. "What exactly do you want me to respect? What kind of military are you even? I don't know anyone in the military that would willingly shoot unarmed citizens," she whispered.

James walked over and put his hand on her shoulder. "Forgive my friend," he said. "Your guys hit her head pretty hard back there."

The sergeant winced and fell silent. The colonel's face grew red. "You are nothing but a spoiled brat. Look at all this trouble they went through to ensure you would survive. Now you are going to complain about it? While we are all here working hard to clean up the surface for you all to live in this new, better world."

Katrina pushed James' hand off her shoulder. "You can keep your world. I don't want any part of this."

"Enough." The colonel slammed his hand on the table. "You don't have another option. I've already spoken with Shelter 17 and they said you all left because you didn't want to follow the rules there either. I'm done playing games with spoiled children."

"Wait, sir. How many shelters are there?" Dreya asked.

"Plenty. More than enough, I say. So many that once you all start doing your jobs, we will be able to weed out any trouble makers." He turned to Katrina again. "You are nothing more than cattle. You don't get any more say in the matter." He walked back to the hall. "Throw them into the holding cells for now."

A group of men came filing through the door and grabbed the kids by their arms. Katrina looked to James and saw his fists clench.

"Please don't resist," said the woman with the bun. "We aren't going to hurt you." Dreya began to walk calmly between two of the men and the rest of the group followed.

Chapter 14

The holding cell was a cement cage with long metal bars separating three rooms from each other and the front walls. There was a single toilet and water fountain in each section. The guards put Jayden and James in one of the cells and the girls in the adjoining one. Metal benches bolted to the floor lined the walls. The woman with the bun tossed in some dark grey wool blankets.

"Just sit tight," she said as she was leaving. "We will get you all sorted out soon."

"What are they going to do with us?" Mia asked after the woman left.

"I think they will probably take us back to the shelter," Jayden said sitting down on the bench. James walked to the far corner of the cell. Katrina watched him for a moment. Then she pulled a blanket over her lap and closed her eyes.

What is happening right now? she thought. These should be the good guys, but they are definitely not the good guys. If I would have gone alone then I would have been in the cabin by now. And my dad would have come. He could explain this. Explain how the government turned on its own people. James is mad and he should be. If we would have just kept running, then we could have gotten away. Away from this messed up world they are building. Where we are, what did the colonel say? Cattle. Livestock. We are just here to breed. To repopulate. Why would my dad put me there? If he is still alive, he might be one of them now. Her stomach churned and a tear escaped from her closed eyes. She pulled the blanket over her head.

Katrina remembered being a little girl standing on her dad's feet as he waltzed her around the living room dancing to Patsy Cline. He was always so sure of himself. Always prepared, always doing the right thing no matter what.

Realization hit her like a ton of bricks.

He wouldn't have made it. He would have fought this, and they would have taken him down. That was why he wasn't there when the doors opened. He had given her a chance at survival with the cabin and she had blown it. She wiped her eyes and snuggled deeper under the blanket. I won't blow it again, she thought.

*

Katrina jerked herself awake. The sun had set, and she could see the night sky through the sliver of a window across the hall from the cage. The lights had dimmed, and it was colder in the room. Her head pain had eased to a dull throbbing ache. Still, she sat up carefully.

Dreya and Mia were huddled together on the bench opposite from hers. She turned to look into the guys cell just as Dreya said, "They took James a few hours ago."

"What?" Katrina jumped to her feet. "Where? Why? Why didn't you wake me up?"

"He said to let you sleep." Dreya peeled herself away from her little sister and tiptoed over to Katrina. "They needed to ask him some questions they said."

Katrina ran to the bars and screamed, "Hey! Where is James? Bring him…"

"Shhh!" Dreya pulled her back down. "It's the middle of the night. They need sleep too." She motioned toward her sister and Jayden. "He will be okay."

"And what if he isn't?" Katrina glared at her. "What if they find out that he wasn't supposed to be in the shelter?"

Dreya smiled softly. "I'm pretty sure they already know that. Why else would they just take him for questioning?"

Katrina's heart was pounding out of her chest. "I don't want to do this without him."

"I know." Dreya wrapped her arms around Katrina to hug her. "We can't do anything about it right now. Hopefully things will look better tomorrow."

Katrina stared at the cracks in the cement wall until the sun rose.

*

The woman with the bun came in with the man carrying the breakfast trays. Katrina screamed at her when she entered. "Go get him and bring him back right now!"

"It's okay sweetie," the woman smiled. "They pulled his records and found out that he does have the dandelion gene. They are just trying to figure out how he got a ticket into the shelter in the first place."

"Who the hell cares?" Katrina continued to shout. "Bring him back in here."

The sergeant walked into the room. "Quit your yelling girl," he said as he smacked his baton across the bars. "You sound like your father calling cadence."

Katrina froze. "What do you know about my dad?"

"I know your file says you are Sgt. Major Floyd's daughter. I took his survival class years ago. I can see where you get your temper from," he laughed.

"My dad was never angry unless you deserved it," she spat.

The sergeant chuckled as he rubbed his chin. "Well maybe I did," he smiled. "You should have said who you were from the beginning. We would have gotten you back home faster."

Mia looked around. "And where is home exactly?"

The sergeant turned his smile to her. "Back to the shelter of course."

"I'm not going anywhere. Not until James is here. And we are definitely not going back to the shelter."

"Oh, you will." The sergeant dropped his smile as he stared at Katrina. "In fact, if you want to see your boyfriend again, you are all going to go back peacefully like the good little boys and girls you are."

*

Hours later, James was escorted back to the cage. He walked with his head hung down.

"You okay man?" Jayden asked, rushing to his side.

Katrina climbed up on the bench next to the bars that separated them. "James?" she whispered. He turned to face her and smiled with a busted lip. She covered her mouth with her hands.

He walked over to sit beside her. "It's okay," he told her while pushing his forehead against hers through the bars. "They just wanted info that I didn't have." He let out a small laugh. "They thought I might be a spy or something, but it turns out I have the dandelion gene too and Morgan somehow rigged the system to get me in. I don't think that I took anyone else's place so that's a relief."

Katrina shook her head. "I don't know what to do anymore. They are sending us back to the fallout shelter."

James smiled again. "Hey. Don't worry so much. Now we just get to do this all over again."

Chapter 15

The colonel came to escort them out as they headed to the truck that would take them back to where it all started.

"Special treatment, huh?" Jayden mumbled with his eyes cast down to the dirt.

"You're damn right kid. Only the best for Sgt. Major Floyd's daughter here." He clapped Katrina on the back.

"You guys keep saying that like you know something that I don't." Katrina stopped walking to look at him.

The colonel smiled. "Just showing some appreciation for the man who helped set up Project Dandelion." Katrina's eyes flashed wide, but she said nothing. "What?" Col. Adams continued. "I thought you would have known that. Didn't you sit through his survival training program in there?" Katrina looked to her feet.

"About that," Dreya asked. "Why teach us survival if we aren't allowed to leave?"

"Floyd's idea," Col. Adams said. "He argued that the mission would need to continue whether we all made it on the surface or not. Thankfully, we did so you don't need to worry. But just in case, you kids had a chance to make it without us here to clean up the mess. Smart man, your father is." He held out his arm to motion Katrina forward.

She climbed into the back of the truck and he pushed the tailgate up after her. "Wait, Colonel," she called out as he began to walk away. "You said "is". Do you know where he is?"

Col. Adams shrugged. "Rumor has it that they moved him to the embassy for the World Headquarters at the new capital in what used to be Maine. Lucky S.O.B."

Katrina sat down hard on the seat as the truck started to drive away.

*

"Man. I was hoping we'd never have to see this place again," Jayden said as they pulled onto the dirt road leading back to the shelter. Through the back of the truck, they saw the desert mostly unchanged since they had left. Ash still covered the earth, but the roads had been cleaned from the multiple tires that had traveled on them.

Katrina groaned as they passed the platform where their parents had dropped them off to take the bus to the shelter on the night the world exploded. "Me too."

*

They didn't see the shelter until they had climbed out of the truck. Katrina wasn't expecting to find anything more than the two tunnels that were dug to the surface, one of which they used to escape. She was shocked to see jarring white tents that sharply contrasted with the greyish ash and desert browns. Military vehicles stood parked to the side and soldiers wearing green jumpsuits while holding rifles mulled about underneath the tents.

"It looks like they got their wish. They are definitely safe now," James smirked.

"Are you sure this is the right kind of safe?" Dreya asked in disgust.

The kids walked into the compound led by the truck driver and another guard. The men they passed quickly stood at attention and then lazily walked away when the driver dismissed them. It was cold under the tents. Colder than should have been possible in the heat of the desert summer. Katrina shivered.

Shea and Christopher from the agriculture group were standing at the back of the main tent talking with some of the guards in jumpsuits. When they looked up to see Katrina, they quickly looked back down to the ground and asked to be excused. They hurried away down a tunnel. Six tunnels dug into the earth circled the outside of the tent compound. The main tent structure they were standing under was built in the center of the tunnels, right on top of where the common room should be buried. Katrina slowly dug her heel into the dirt. She really didn't want to go back down there.

The kids stood there waiting as the guards walked about. The guards were busy doing much of nothing. Two men and a petite woman leaned against the outside of the main tent laughing at something the woman said. Others were inspecting vehicles and digging holes out in the desert. Another woman stood with a clipboard directing soldiers to move supplies around in the storage tent. There was an air of boredom and impatience. Katrina watched them move about like bees on a lazy spring afternoon. It would have almost been peaceful had the men not been armed.

These were military members, Katrina thought. But something is off about them. Not just the weird uniforms, but something different. She couldn't place her finger on it. Scanning the tents and then the horizon, she realized there was no flag. There were no emblems on the uniforms showing the branch of service. Who were these people?

"Ugh, guys," Mia whispered bringing Katrina out of her thoughts. "Why does Lark have a gun?"

Chapter 16

From behind a screened off section of the tent, the blond boy with a politician's smile came strutting towards the group of kids. His hair was shorter, and he was wearing the simple green uniform the rest of the guards were wearing. A rifle was slung across his back held on by a leather strap. He still had the same cold brown eyes and the same set to his shoulders. Katrina's stomach turned.

Was he taller? Katrina thought. Something was different about him. Her vision blurred as she tried to take in the slightly distorted image.

"Well there are my runaway children," he laughed as he approached. His voice was different too. "What's wrong?" He stopped short. "You all look like you've seen a ghost."

Dreya stared at him. Her face was pale. "You look just like him," she whispered. "Just like Lark."

The guy beamed his smile at her. "I guess genetically I should look like him. Lark's my cousin. He is the reason I asked to be assigned here. The name's Lieutenant Bayer," he said extending his hand. "And your name is?"

"Dreya." She firmly crossed her arms over her chest.

Lt. Bayer's smile crept up to his eyes. "Dreya you say? Well I know Lark is going to be happy that you are back. And this must be your little sister Mia." He winked at her. "She looks just like you too. And this..." He stepped back and spread his arms. "This must be Katrina. The infamous Sgt. Major Floyd's daughter. The girl who broke my cousin's nose. Now we aren't going to have any more trouble from you, are we sweetheart?"

"Not as long as no one ties me up again," Katrina said through clenched teeth.

Lt. Bayer raised his eyebrows as he looked at her. James instinctively moved closer to Katrina's side. "And you must be the boyfriend," Lt. Bayer stepped back. "Good. That's good. Have at it. That's all we want you kids to do. Stay healthy. Fall in love. Create a family. Why don't you all head back down to your room now? Have fun." He looked back to Katrina. "I'll be up here if you need me."

Bile rose up in the back of Katrina's throat as the puzzle pieces connected. The way Lark smiled when Nanny had explained about the dandelion gene on the first day. How he had tried to take advantage of Anna. Trying to make everyone stay there- he knew. He knew what was happening all along. And he knew he would get what he wanted. Katrina's stomach hurt. How did she not see that?

They were directed back to the tunnel that led down to Room 3. The graded steps that James had carefully dug out had blocks of lumber with rebar stakes through the wood to hold them in place. Katrina stood at the top of the hole and inhaled a deep breath of radioactive tainted fresh air before she descended into the bunker again.

*

The room looked smaller than she remembered. It took a second for her eyes to adjust even though the fluorescent lights were burning bright. Everything was the same as the first day they had arrived. The metal bunks had new mattresses and blankets on them. Katrina smiled as she thought of how they had torn up the beds to make waterproof packs from the plastic mattress liners before they left.

Ethan was sitting alone in the room on his bunk. He jumped up smiling as they entered. "You're back," he laughed as Dreya went to hug him. "They said you were coming back but I didn't want to believe it. How was it out there?"

"Bad," Dreya said walking over to her old bunk. "Really bad. They are killing off anyone left alive. I guess this whole thing is some sort of diabolical plan to start a new world with one government."

Ethan nodded. "Yeah, we've heard about that plan. They didn't tell us the rest of it, but I figured as much. Did you guys hear that we are livestock? This whole Project Dandelion thing was just a way to keep us alive to repopulate the earth with loyal subjects to the new world order. Fun, huh? And if they think we need help accomplishing that mission well…" His voice trailed off as he looked to James and Jayden. "They are making me take gentleman classes because I'm not so good with the ladies."

"What are gentleman classes?" Mia asked as she sat on the bed beside Ethan.

"It's just this stupid class they are doing. They took away our survival class in the morning and now we get an hour of propaganda class before we break into different groups. I have to go to the gentleman class which is basically a bunch of frat guys trying to tell me how to get a girl. Lieutenant Bayer runs it."

"Of course he does." Katrina rolled her eyes.

"I should have left with you all," Ethan said to her. "I'm sorry that I stayed."

"Don't be." Mia patted his back gently. "We just got dragged right back here anyway."

"How is Willow handling all of this?" Jayden asked as he took the bunk on top of Ethan's.

"Why don't you ask me yourself?" Willow said as she walked through the doorway. Ethan smiled at her and she warmly smiled back.

Katrina was confused. "Are you guys together now?"

"No!" they both shouted in unison.

"I mean no," Willow said softly while leaning against the doorframe. "We were just all that was left of Room 3 when you guys took off. It was a rough few days of questioning when the military showed up. They wanted to know where you went, but since we weren't privileged to any of the details, they let us off the hook."

"Oh my gosh." Dreya sat down on her bed. "I'm so sorry that happened to you. We didn't know what was actually happening up there when we left."

"None of us did." Willow brushed her off. "Well, you are back now. How was your vacation?"

"It's bad," Dreya told her. "They are killing anyone who survived."

"I guess that's what happens in war." Willow shrugged and a distant look colored her eyes. "I wish it wasn't like this, but we can't change anything now, can we?"

"And you're okay with that?" James asked her.

"What else are we going to do? I mean they are trying this new government thing. They want to make the world a better place. This is just the hard part, the beginning."

"Are you serious?" Mia snapped at her. "Tell me you are joking."

Willow glared at her as the dinner packets dropped into the cabinet. "That's my cue," she said, leaving the room. "I'm staying in Room 5 now. Figured you all would want to stick together."

Dreya took out the food bags quickly to stop the alarm from beeping. "I really didn't miss that sound," she said as she handed the bags around the room.

Mia groaned. "I really didn't miss eating MREs for every meal. I almost wish we had more marmot to eat."

"You ate a marmot?" Ethan gulped.

Katrina laughed. "We will tell you all about our adventures."

*

"Do you want to go see the movie tonight?" Jayden asked Dreya after dinner.

"Might as well," she sighed while getting up. "It's not like we have anything better to do."

The six of them walked down the dimly lit tunnel which led to the common room. Katrina held her breath waiting for the angry mob of kids to confront them as they entered. She stood closer to James as she remembered how easily they had all turned against Room 3 and had allowed her to be tied up in Lark's room. *I should have stayed in bed tonight*, she thought.

James grabbed her hand as they rounded the corner. The gym was full. All the kids were settling down on the bleachers or sitting on the floor for the movie. No one had their mattresses out though. A few guards stood leaning against the walls. All eyes turned towards Room 3 as they entered.

Katrina noticed Peter and Juan first, the brothers who had joined the labor group. They gave her a silent nod before turning back to watch the screen. More smiles directed towards her and her friends played across many of the kids' faces before they quickly turned away. James looked to Katrina with his eyebrows raised.

She shook her head in disbelief. "I guess they are happy we are home," she whispered.

Lark wasn't there and neither was Anthony or Brett. Becca was sitting with a group of girls, but she walked over to sit next to Dreya when the movie started.

"I'm sorry," she said as she sat on the bleachers. "You were right about Lark." Becca turned back to face Katrina. "I should have listened."

Dreya squeezed her hand. "It's alright. There are things we all should have done differently. How are you?"

Becca shook her head as she looked to the guards and back. "Can we talk more tomorrow?" she asked. Dreya nodded and they watched *Toy Story 4* unfold on the projector screen.

*

After her roommates had fallen asleep, Katrina leaned down from her bunk to find James lying in his bed underneath her still awake. She nodded toward the bathroom. They tiptoed over and he quietly closed the door behind them.

Katrina slid down against the wall to sit on the cold tile floor and pulled her knees to her chest. James sat down beside her. They stared into the silence for a few moments until James chuckled.

"You know, I feel like we don't talk anymore."

Katrina looked at him. "Well we spent the last few weeks just trying to survive. It's not like when we were stuck down here. We haven't had any time."

"I know," he smiled at her. "You used to be able to take a joke."

Katrina groaned and put her head against her knees. "Are you still mad at me?" she asked.

"No," he said. "It was a stupid decision. If we just kept running, we would have been there by now. But I know why you had to go back and to be honest, it would have eaten me up in the long run if we hadn't."

"Thanks," she said lifting her head, "for understanding. Except I don't even understand myself anymore. My head is all messed up."

"Yeah," James nodded. "That's nothing new though, it always kind of was. Plus, you got hit on it pretty hard."

"Seriously," she glared at him. "Not now."

"Okay, okay. Talk to me. Tell me where you are at."

"This whole thing is wrong. I grew up with the military. They are the good guys. How did they let this happen? They are shooting civilians, killing innocent people, and supporting this crazy new government. And now it seems like my dad was in on this or was a part of the whole thing. He knew what Project Dandelion was and he put me down here anyway."

"Well you did say that he told you this would be the safest place…"

"Yeah, but it isn't. The safest place would have been with him somewhere. He knew this was coming, and by the sound of it he knew exactly what this was that was coming. I'm so confused. I don't know which way is up or down anymore."

James smiled. "That's okay. I know where we are. I know we are down here, and you are right here next to me. We are pretty sure your dad is up there, somewhere. And if he is all that you say he is, I'll bet he had a plan to keep you safe. Now we need to have a plan," he laughed. "I guess a new plan. So, stop sulking and let's come up with one."

Her eyes welled up with tears as she looked at him. "You know, my dad would really like you."

"Of course he would," James winked. "What's not to like?"

James caught her chin with the palm of his hand as she started laughing. He tilted her head up slightly and leaned down to kiss her. Katrina closed her eyes as he closed the distance between their lips.

"Don't do this if you are going to stop so soon again," she whispered.

He paused and she opened her eyes. The laughter faded and his eyes turned murky blue. "One day I'm hoping there won't be a reason to break away." He kissed her forehead. "Now isn't the time."

Katrina groaned as he stood up. You stupid girl, she thought. I shouldn't have said anything.

He extended his hand to pull her up. "First we have to get out of here, again."

Chapter 17

"Welcome to day 29 in the shelter."

Mia threw her shoe at the loudspeaker and missed. "I could have gone the rest of my life without ever hearing Nanny announce the days again," she yelled.

"We have to go," Ethan said after breakfast. "They don't let us miss class or their new exercise session anymore. If it's a good air quality day, we get to go outside. I'm not sure if that's better or worse."

*

Everyone sat quietly on the bleachers before the lecture started. Guards filled the gym. Lark sat across the room with Anthony and Brett. He glared at Katrina as she entered. The projection that played on the screen wasn't the normal one directed by Nanny. Instead, music blared as a flag depicting a Pangea with all the continents connected inside a red circle blew in the breeze aboard a ship. The kids were required to stand and raise their arm in respect. Ethan motioned to the guards as he nudged Dreya and urged the rest of them to join in. Katrina slowly raised her arm but kept her middle finger extended and pressed behind her back.

An old woman with yellow teeth and a blue blazer came on the screen. She smiled at the camera.

"Good morning children." A translator furiously spoke in multiple languages as the woman paused. "We are still out here working hard to make the world a better place for you. We must clear out all the things that would harm you or stand in the way of you living a happy life." She paused again. "Our number one mission has been, and has always been, ensuring that you are safe and taken care of. I know this is scary and confusing, but I can promise you that it will make more sense in the coming years. When you have families of your own soon, they will be in a unified world that works together for the common good."

Her teeth shone more golden as the sun reflected from them. "You are our hope for humanity, and we know that each of you are strong enough to adapt to that role. The new Republic of the Earth loves you and you must love us. We just need a little more time and we will get you out of those shelters and into someplace better. A place where you can grow, our beautiful dandelions."

The screen cut out to a map of the world with zones marked "cleared". Then a man in a lab coat came on as he discussed weather patterns and how the fallout was starting to disintegrate.

Katrina leaned down to Ethan. "Who was that woman?"

He shook his head. "It's been the same recording of her for three days. Before that it was a Russian man for about a week which they translated for us." A guard across the room smacked his baton against the wall and put his finger over his lips. Ethan faced the front.

After the lesson, the kids broke into groups. Ethan and a couple of the other boys went over to Lt. Bayer's group. A small woman with her blond hair cut delicately above her ears came over to talk with the rest of Room 3. "We haven't quite figured out where you all need to be in your lessons yet so you can all follow me to the child birth class."

"Um," Mia took a step back. "No thank you. I am way too young and way too innocent to learn anything about childbirth."

The woman laughed. "I promise it is not gruesome and you'll have a few years before anyone expects you to give birth. Think of it as more like a reproductive health class. It never hurts to be informed."

The woman, Dr. Clark who insisted the kids call her Dr. C, began the discussion by going over how the female body functioned. Katrina only half listened as she was fairly confident that she knew how it worked. Glancing around the room, she saw Ethan standing in a circle of guards. His face was beet red and the men were laughing at him. Five other boys stood outside of the circle nervously shifting from foot to foot. Lt. Bayer caught her staring and winked at her. She quickly looked down to her feet. Her stomach was in knots again.

When she looked back up, she saw Lark and his cronies along with Samantha from agriculture and two other guys leaving down Tunnel 6 with some of the guards.

"They are in the military training group," Becca whispered as she slid over next to Katrina. "They volunteered to do it. The training is on the surface."

"Why aren't you with them?" Katrina whispered back.

"Because I don't want to have any babies."

"Why would you take this class then?" Katrina turned to face her.

Becca stared straight ahead. "It's safer here where no one is trying to win any awards. If I would have stayed in that group, I would have had to get pregnant and I'm definitely not ready to do that."

Katrina shook her head, her face aghast. "Did he do anything to you?"

"No," Becca smirked. "But what he did to Anna, he did it because he knew he could get away with it. He knew what this was all along."

"Ladies," Dr. C called out to Becca and Katrina. "I know you think you know all this already, but a refresher course is important too. Please pay attention or I'll have to send you to work crew." The girls nodded and followed along with the rest of the lesson.

*

The exercise session was on the surface. Katrina couldn't wait to get some real air, tainted with radiation or not. The guards, led by Lt. Bayer, ran a military style PT session for the kids complete with pushups, whistles, and lots of screaming. Katrina was dripping with sweat as the guards ran them around the dirt track that had been pounded out by feet during the exercise sessions they had missed.

When she thought she might faint, the guards blew the whistle to announce hygiene time. As she made her way to the tunnel a shoulder slammed against her almost knocking her down. She spun around to see Lark glaring at her while walking backwards. His cold eyes pierced through the yellow and purplish bruising that spread across his cheekbones. Katrina chuckled as she went to catch up with James.

"What's so funny?" he asked her as they walked into the room.

"Lark is still pretty upset with me," she giggled as she climbed on top of her bed. "You should see his face up close."

*

That night as they were getting ready for bed, Becca poked her head into the room and nodded to Ethan. He jumped up and ran over to the door that led outside. After he slightly cracked it to look outside, he gave Becca a thumbs up and then closed the door again. Becca motioned for the others to join her in the hallway.

"They disengaged the locks somehow," she explained. "They can come in whenever they want. It's safer to meet in the tunnels. Supposedly we are allowed to do whatever we want during our own time but if they get suspicious that we are plotting anything we get in trouble." Peter, Juan, Laura, and Marie were waiting in the hall. "Stay there by the door," Becca said. "So you can run back to bed quickly if Ethan calls."

"What's this about?" Jayden asked.

"We need help," Becca sighed. "We have been trying to come up with a plan to overthrow these thugs, but we really need your help to do it."

James laughed. "What's wrong with the society that they are building for you? It sounds a lot like what you were trying to do before we left." Becca glared at him.

Marie put her hand on her hip. "Hello. Have you seen what they are trying to make us do? We are just breeding stock to them. They are going to make us have kids in a few years and we are supposed to raise them to follow this government's every order. This is not at all what I had in mind when I thought about starting a family. And have you seen the gene pool that we have to choose from here? If I'm the one that has to do all the work of having children, they should at least have given me better options." She crossed her arms as she glanced to Peter and Juan. "No offense guys."

Peter smiled. "None taken." He turned to James. "We never really cared about this society anyway. We just didn't have any other plan on what to do. Sticking together seemed the best idea. Now anything else sounds better than this. This isn't my country they are building."

"We wouldn't be the only ones to fight back either," Laura nodded. "Some of the guards were talking about another uprising in Shelter 23 or something. They were scared."

Katrina put her hand on James' bicep. He locked eyes with her, and they stepped back into the shadows as the rest of the kids talked.

"This could be it," she whispered to him. "This could be the plan."

"It's too risky." James shook his head. "They have guns and we don't."

"But we have to try," she pleaded with him. "If it goes sour, we can always try to escape in the commotion."

James exhaled. "Bad plan, but I'll try it with you."

Katrina smiled and they rejoined the group. She nodded to Dreya and Jayden.

"Okay," Jayden said. "We are in. What do we need to do?"

Becca clapped her hands. "Nothing just yet," she said. "We need Dreya first."

"Me?" Dreya looked confused.

"We need everyone on board before we can strike. Obviously Lark and his friends won't join us. But we still have ten other kids on the fence down here. They don't trust me to lead them, but they did follow you Dreya. If you can be the face of the uprising, they might join our side. Then we can all work together to bring down the guards." Becca winked at her. "We need you, mom."

Chapter 18

"Why do you always do this?" Mia screamed at her older sister after they closed the door to the room.

"Always do what?" Dreya asked her.

Katrina started laughing as she and James climbed into their bunks. "She does always do this," Katrina said. "She can't help it though, it's just who she is."

"What exactly do I always do?" Dreya stood by the door. "Help if I'm needed?"

"It's more than helping," Mia said as she sat on her bed. "You always get too involved. You make everyone else's problems your own. You always have to be the leader."

"I didn't ask for this," Dreya told her. "If I see a need for someone to step up, I will. Do you want me to say no?"

"And hear about it for the rest of my life? No thanks. Do whatever you want." Mia put the pillow over her face.

Dreya looked around the room and Katrina smiled encouragingly at her before lying down. "I didn't want any of this, but since we are here, I might as well do something."

"I know babe," Jayden chuckled. "It's just who you are."

Mia groaned from under her blankets.

*

During hygiene the following day, Katrina went with Dreya and Becca to the girls in Room 5. Laura and Marie pushed Anna, Willow, Sarah, and Carol into the hall.

"Not this again," Willow said as soon as she saw Becca. "I'm not fighting against the guards."

"We aren't even going to have to really fight." Becca leaned against the wall. "They aren't supposed to hurt us. We are their livestock. They are supposed to protect us."

"Yeah but they can make life miserable for us," Sarah said. "Even more miserable than it is right now."

"What's the point?" Willow crossed her arms. "The world is crap out there and it may be bad here, but like you said we are safe here at least."

"Don't you want to be in charge of your own lives?" Katrina asked. "Don't you want to make your own choices?"

"We are choosing," Sarah laughed. "We are choosing not to make a dumb decision that could hurt us."

"What if there was a place that we could take you?" Dreya interrupted.

Katrina's heart beat faster as she stared at Dreya. Don't tell them about the cabin, Katrina screamed in her head.

Dreya smiled at her as she continued, "We found a paradise when we were out there. A place in the mountains with clean air and clean water. There are fish and rabbits and the government doesn't know anything about it. We can take you there and away from here. You can live there and build the society that you really wanted. It will be safe. You'd just have to help us all get past the guards. We could leave. We could take their guns and their trucks. Then we could go to our own paradise and they wouldn't be able to find us."

The girls were silent. Katrina didn't take her eyes off Dreya.

"Can you promise we will get there?" Carol asked.

"I'll die trying." Dreya looked to her. "But yes, I can get you there."

Sarah looked around at the rest of the girls. "Screw it," she shrugged. "It's a bad plan, but why not try? What do you think Carol?"

"I guess if no one gets hurt, it would be worth a try. The clean water and fishing sounds good to me." Carol smiled.

Becca let out her breath. "And what about you Anna? You've been awfully quiet through all of this."

Anna blushed. "I've had a lot of time to think. I have always wanted what was best for everyone and for us to all just get along. I liked the idea of building a society where we could work together. But what they are doing, what the government or whoever they are now is doing, this isn't right. They are forcing us to accept it like we tried to make you guys do. Sorry about that by the way. And I don't want to accept this." Anna looked up from the floor as she smiled. "This is Lark's world now and I don't want to be a part of that world."

Dreya laughed and pulled Anna in for a hug. "I'm so glad you figured out that you were better than that guy. You are so much stronger than him. No one has the right to force anyone to do anything they don't want to. Except Lark, we should totally force that guy to eat dirt."

Anna giggled as she peeled Dreya's arms off her. "Alright. But I still don't want to fight. Can you figure out a job that I can do that doesn't hurt anyone?" Dreya nodded as Becca turned toward Willow again.

"What are you thinking Willow?" Dreya asked. "Are you with us?"

Willow looked to her friends. "Ugh," she sighed. "Whatever you guys want." She turned to Dreya. "I'm still mad at you for pushing me out of the room but I understand now why you did it. I'm with you Dreya. But I'm not eating any rabbits."

*

Becca practically went skipping down the hall. Katrina pulled Dreya's arm back and furiously whispered to her.

"What the hell were you thinking? We can't take them up there. How will they even survive if they get there?"

Dreya smiled reassuringly. "I had to give them something. They need hope. I will figure out a way to get them there, without compromising you or the cabin I promise. Once I get them there, they can figure out the rest. I'm still going with you. It will just be a pit stop that we have to make."

"This is not a good idea," Katrina huffed.

"I'm still working out the details," Dreya sighed. "But you know this is the right thing to do."

Katrina nodded and started walking but Dreya held her back. "Hey, do me a favor and don't tell Mia," Dreya pleaded. "Give me some time to find the right words so she doesn't freak out."

Katrina smiled. "Oh, she is going to freak out no matter how you say it."

Chapter 19

Lark and his roommates were hanging out in the common room.

"What were you doing down there?" Lark asked Becca as Katrina and Dreya followed her out of the tunnel.

"Just girl stuff." Becca shrugged. "What are you guys doing out here? Shouldn't you be showering or something?" Anthony and Brett laughed.

"Bet you wish he was showering." Brett blew a kiss to Becca. Katrina could barely see Anthony's face through the discoloration of the fading bruises. James got him good, she thought. Becca's cheeks turned red and she stomped off toward Tunnel 2.

"Hang on a second," Lark called. Becca stopped. "Not you Becca. We already know where you stand. I want to talk to Dreya."

Becca looked back to the girls and Dreya nodded for her to go. Becca kept walking.

"What do you want?" Dreya's voice was cold.

"I just want to talk to you." Lark's eyes traveled to Katrina. "Alone, if you don't mind."

Katrina crossed her arms over her chest. "I'm not going anywhere. If you want to talk, start talking."

Lark leaned back against the bleachers and sighed. "You still plan on being a trouble maker?" Katrina stared at him. "I'd watch my step if I were you. There are serious consequences if you don't behave now. One call to my cousin and I can have you out of here." His smile didn't reach his eyes.

Katrina bit her tongue as Dreya laughed. "Yeah. We already met Lt. Bayer. It seems like he has a thing for Katrina though. I'm not sure how strong that threat of yours is," Dreya said.

Lark snorted. "It's not a threat. Just stating facts. Anyway, they don't get a choice or a chance at love. We do." He winked at Dreya. "Speaking of that, is Jayden still following you around like a lost puppy?"

"Jayden is fine. Thank you for asking." Dreya smiled.

Lark put his hands behind his head. "Hmm. Well let me know when you want to get with a real man. I'm looking for a strong woman to have my future children with." Katrina's jaw dropped open and she started to respond as Dreya stepped forward.

"A real man! That's what you think you are? You are nothing more than a spoiled child who thinks he can take anything that he wants. You disgust me. Anna was right, this is your world now. A world where everyone is forced to take a crappy deal just to survive. You can shove your world right up your…"

Katrina pulled Dreya back and tried to guide her toward the tunnel.

"I'd be careful what you say, sweetheart," Lark yelled after her. "You wouldn't want my cousin to think you girls were up to no good."

Katrina turned to face him after she got Dreya to calm down. "You aren't going to say anything to cause problems because if you do, you'll never stand a chance with her."

Lark smiled and blew a kiss. Katrina caught Dreya as she lunged forward and dragged her down Tunnel 3 with the sounds of the boys' laughter echoing behind them.

*

Before they reached the door, Katrina put her hand on Dreya's shoulder. "You okay?" she whispered.

Dreya nodded. "I can't believe I snapped like that. This place makes me feel crazy. I really hate that guy."

Katrina laughed. "I completely understand. We all hate him." Dreya took a deep breath as they entered the room.

"How was it?" Jayden asked climbing down from his bed.

"It went good," Dreya said calmly. "The girls are all in with us."

"Of course they are." Jayden smiled at her. "You are a Rockstar. How could they say no to you?"

Dreya ran across the room and grabbed Jayden's face in her hands. She gave him a long smoldering kiss and pulled away leaving him breathless.

"Eeww," Mia yelled throwing her pillow at them. "Get a room why don't you?"

James saw Katrina's face as she walked to her bunk. "What really happened?" he whispered.

She shook her head. "I'll tell you later."

*

The two boys from agriculture were tougher to crack than the girls had been.

"Tell me again how we are supposed to grow crops on the side of a glacier in this paradise of yours," Shea said.

Katrina sat on the floor of the hallway next to Dreya and sighed. "You probably can't grow them on that side of the mountain but a little below in the next valley or maybe on the opposite slope would work."

"Without seeing the terrain ourselves, how do we know it would work? You said the water is clean.

Did you test it? How do you know that it is safe?" Christopher asked.

Dreya leaned her head against her knees. "We drank it and we aren't dead."

Christopher shook his head. "That is a horrible study and we still don't know the results. You could drop dead tomorrow."

Katrina stretched her back out against the wall to crack it. "It's not like you would be able to grow anything out here in the desert."

"Well we don't technically have to grow anything here. Out there we will," Shea leaned against the door frame.

"Oh my gosh." Dreya raised her head to look at him. "We just keep going in circles with this. Will you guys fight with us or not?"

Christopher touched Shea's bicep and whispered in his ear. Katrina saw Shea's sly smile to Christopher that quickly disappeared as he looked forward.

"We'll fight," Shea nodded. "We just want to know what we are fighting for."

"The right to choose how you want to live your own life," Katrina said standing up. "You are fighting for freedom."

*

"Welcome to day 31 in the shelter," Nanny's voice echoed her familiar morning salutation. The fluorescent lights burned Katrina's eyes, so she pulled the pillow over her face.

James lifted it away from her as he handed her the breakfast packet. "Time to get up, sleeping beauty. We don't want to be late to Brain Washing 101."

Chapter 20

There was an uneasy commotion in the common room as they entered that morning. Becca was standing near the bleachers with Laura and Marie. She walked over to Dreya when she came out of the tunnel.

"One of the guards said we get a new announcement today," Becca whispered. Katrina saw that the back wall of the gym was lined with more guards than there were the previous morning. Lt. Bayer stood in the center of a group of men. He smiled at her when she caught his eye and she quickly looked away as she reached for James' hand. James looked at her quizzically and she shook her head as they made their way to the seats.

The music played and the flag waved across the screen. A young woman with curling red hair tied back in a ponytail stood on the deck of a ship in port. There were green mountains in the background. Hawaii maybe? Or New Zealand? Katrina strained to make them out. It's definitely an island somewhere, she thought.

The woman spoke with a heavy British accent. "Good morning our lovely dandelions. Today is a day for the history books. As of this morning, we have received word that over 75% of the earth has been cleared by our strategically placed military units. We have cleaned up most of the continent formally known as Asia and well as portions of what was Africa and most of the old North American and South American continents. New zones are being marked clear hourly."

She paused to smile while the translator caught up. "The weather has also shifted faster than we anticipated. In many places, the most dangerous of the fallout is dissipating at astronomical rates. Phase one of our plan was to keep you all safe because you are our future. I am happy to announce that very soon, phase two will begin. This phase will be reentry. I promise there will be more information in the coming days. Soon you will be on the surface and we can get you settled into your new lives under the World Republic. These lives will be rich in community and secure under the new order." The woman was practically bouncing out of her skin with excitement. "Sources tell us that the rest of the old North America and most of Europe should be cleared by the end of the week. Your time to bloom is coming soon little dandelions." The projection ended.

Katrina looked around the room. The other kids sat stone faced staring at the blank screen. A few of the guards began to furiously whisper to one another. Lt. Bayer smacked his baton against the wall and all the guards jumped to attention.

Lt. Bayer smiled as he walked to the center of the room. He stopped to pat Lark on the back before he addressed the kids. "Celebrate, dandelions." He clapped his hands together. "You are getting out of here soon."

The teens began to dutifully clap. Katrina moved her hands in the motion but didn't make a noise. She glanced over to see Dr. C leaning against the wall near Tunnel 2. Dr. C looked pale as she slowly clapped along. Katrina looked back to see all the guards gathered together in the common room. The room spun into sharp focus as the plan to escape came to her. She just had to work out the details.

A laugh escaped her lips. James looked at her like she was crazy as the room continued to clap.

*

Ethan went with Dreya, Becca, and Katrina to speak with the last four kids from the tech group who didn't want to fight back. The boys followed Ethan out of their room and into the tunnel.

"It's not happening Becca," Byron said as he entered the hall. "Did you hear that this morning? We will have nowhere to go. They are taking over the planet."

"We do have somewhere to go," Dreya smiled but Paul cut her off.

"We've already heard about your paradise," he said. "It won't work. Even if they don't track us there, they have drones. I'm sure they also have control of at least one satellite. They would find us eventually. The smart thing to do is to play by their rules. They are the ones winning."

"They are lying," Katrina said in exasperation. "Did you see how the guards reacted to the news? They are confused because that isn't what they were told. That chic was flat out lying. There is no way they could clear that much of the earth that fast. And all of Asia? You think they could clear the Himalayas in one month? No freaking way. They just want us to think they are winning."

"Still," Nico said. "What's the point in fighting? It is safe here. It might not be safe out there. Do you really want to take your chances going against them? It's suicide."

"But it is a slow painful half-existence if we stay here," Dreya said. "Other shelters have already risen up. If we all do it then we can kill their plans. We can prove that we aren't the easily manipulated kids that they think we are. We can live and die by an idea greater than ourselves, the idea of freedom. The right to freedom and being able to live the life you want. Screw what this government tells you is safe. How do you want to live? What do you think is worth fighting for?"

Simon laughed. "Well I sure as hell don't want to die for an idea. I'll tell you that." The other boys started chuckling and Dreya's cheeks flushed.

Ethan cleared his throat. "We are going to die someday guys. We might as well not go down as cowards."

Simon stopped laughing to look at him. "Give us a while to talk. We'll get back to you."

*

The dinner packets arrived in Room 3.

"We never got chicken fajitas before," Jayden exclaimed as he ripped into the bag. "This is exciting."

Katrina laughed. "Calm down. Seriously. You aren't going to like what you find."

Jayden's eyes were sad as he looked up at her. "Man. Why do you have to crush my dreams?"

"Well the tortillas aren't that bad," Katrina winked as she sat down next to James on the floor.

Ethan walked through the doorway smiling as Dreya handed him his food. "The tech guys are in," he said and sat down to join his roommates for dinner.

Chapter 21

Katrina crept to the bathroom after lights out and James closed the door behind them. "I have a plan," she said as she sat on the counter. "Tell me what you think."

James sat on the floor across from her. "Let's hear it."

"We need to get all the guards down here. We need to trap them all in this coffin and then we can leave."

"That's a good idea," James said. "But it will never work. There are fifty guards up there. They wouldn't be dumb enough to all come down."

"Maybe not. But if we can get a bunch of them in here then we will stand a chance."

"What happens when they call in reinforcements?" James asked.

"We are in the middle of the desert. It will take hours for anyone to get here," she smiled. "And we know the back roads out."

"Okay," James nodded. "This could possibly work. How do we keep them inside? They disengaged the locks. And how do we get us all out?"

"During the movie." Katrina jumped off the counter. "A lot of them will already be down here. We overwhelm them, take their guns, and restrain them. We'll take their radios and call for help. Then more will come down. We will be hiding in the bathrooms and when they run in, we will run out. We'll tie off the doors with sheets."

"And what do we do when we get to the surface?" James raised his eyebrows.

"Geez, do you expect me to think of everything?" she smiled. "We need to rush them in the confusion and steal some trucks. I also need to come up with some sort of distraction during the movie."

James laughed. "I'll take care of the distraction. It is the least I can do." He stood up and took her hand into his. "You know this is a stupid plan, right? We should just escape. It would be harder to track just the two of us. We might actually stand a chance."

Katrina gazed into his eyes. "If you would have talked to me a month ago, I would have said the same thing. Except it is different now. There is, I don't know, an idea I am fighting for. I have to at least try and do the right thing here."

"I know," he smiled. "If we ever do make it to the cabin though, I want you to know that I want more." James leaned down and kissed her on her jawline sending chills into her stomach and causing her heart to race.

"Me too," she whispered as he pulled away and held the bathroom door open for them.

*

Katrina woke before the lights came on in the morning. Ethan's snores echoed through the room and she heard the steady breathing of the rest of her roommates. She pulled the wool blanket up to her chin and touched where James had kissed her last night. She groaned as she rolled to her side.

What do I want? She asked herself. I want more answers. I want to talk to my dad, or do I now? Do I want to find out he had a part in all of this? I want to know why he left me here. I want to get to the cabin. I want James. She smiled at the dream she had been holding of them living peacefully together in the mountains. Maybe they'd have a family someday. She never really wanted kids before, but maybe.

Katrina turned onto her stomach. If she wanted that, why didn't she just stay here? It was what this new world wanted her to do. Except, they weren't giving her a choice. They weren't giving anyone a choice. They took away their free will and expected them to just fall in line for this new world because of what some scientist said about this stupid dandelion gene.

She didn't want to do that. Above all else, she didn't want to just roll over and die. Didn't want to let someone else dictate the life she would live. The right thing to do was to fight back and to help the others fight back too.

The lights blared as Nanny's voice came over the loudspeaker.

Day 32 in the shelter.

Chapter 22

During health class, Dreya whispered the plan to Becca who took it all in smiling. Katrina watched Dr. C glance over at the girls, but she said nothing as they talked. During hygiene time, Katrina stripped the sheets from the beds and stacked them in the bathroom shower. Mia followed her anxiously.

"Are you sure this is going to work?" she asked.

"It's the best plan I have right now," Katrina smiled at the girl. "I sure hope it does."

*

The lights dimmed as *Spiderman* played on the projector screen. Katrina silently tapped her foot on the ground. There were twelve guards leaning against the walls watching the movie as the opening scene played. Three had radios and only two carried rifles. James leaned down to whisper to Jayden and both boys stood up. Katrina inhaled deeply to steady her breath.

"Hey man," Jayden called out as he walked over to Lark. "Yeah you. Get up weasel. I heard you were harassing my girl the other day." James walked beside Jayden.

"What?" Lark said standing as he looked over to Dreya. Anthony and Brett also stood. "I don't know what you are talking about."

"We aren't playing that game this time," Jayden closed the distance between the two of them. "You said you were a real man, huh? Well let's see you fight like one." Jayden shoved him.

"Hey," one of the guards shouted. "Sit down and watch the movie or we are sending you all to bed."

"You hear that?" Jayden asked. "He said sit down." Jayden pushed Lark again and he fell into the bleachers. Lark stood back up and Jayden cold punched him right on his healing nose. Katrina could hear the crunching noise vibrate through the gym over the sounds of the movie.

Anthony and Brett lunged. James and Jayden began to wrestle them.

"Knock it off," the guard yelled as the rest of the men came running forward. One guard reached for his radio and Katrina rushed toward him. The room came alive as the kids jumped from the bleachers and tackled the guards. Katrina grabbed the radio from the guard's hand as Dreya and Becca jumped on him. She turned to see the other kids had ripped away the guns and two remaining radios without a shot being fired.

Dreya directed the kids to tie the guards along with Lark and his friends to the bleachers. Once she had given everyone enough time to get back to their rooms, she walked over to Lark. She held the radio out toward him. "Tell them everything is okay," she whispered. He nodded and she pressed the button for him to speak.

"Lt. Bayer," Lark said calmly as he looked in her eyes. "There has been an uprising. We need immediate assistance. Help!" She clicked off the radio and Lark smiled smugly before spitting on her feet.

"That was great," she smiled at him. "You did exactly what I thought you would. Thanks for all your help." The remainder of Room 3 ran down their tunnel to sit in the bathroom and wait.

*

Katrina heard the boots of the guards running through the room. It sounds like four men, she thought. If they sent down four men to each tunnel there wasn't many on the surface left.

When the guards entered the hall, Jayden and Ethan ran over to secure the door shut. Dreya and Katrina ran to the exit. "Stay behind us Mia!" Dreya shouted as she charged up the tunnel. Katrina stayed on her heels as they sprinted up the steps.

They came up onto the surface of the earth and Katrina saw the heads of kids emerging from all six of the tunnels. The remaining guards began to fire, and a rubber bullet hit Katrina in the shoulder. She was knocked back into James and he helped her out of the hole and onto the ground. Dreya charged a guard and managed to get his rifle from him. James looked Katrina over quickly and then took off running with Jayden to find more of the guards.

Katrina climbed to her feet while holding her left shoulder. The kids had all gotten out and the guards were outnumbered. They were getting them, she thought. She ran behind the central partition to get to the office and found Dr. C sitting behind a desk. They locked eyes.

"Keys," Katrina said. "We need keys to the trucks over there."

"Take the Humvees," Dr. C told her. "They don't need keys."

"They aren't fast enough," Katrina shook her head. "We need to go fast."

Dr. C nodded. "Wait here. I'll go get them." She darted behind the screen. Katrina rubbed her bruised shoulder anxiously for what felt like an eternity.

Dr. C finally reappeared holding three sets of keys. "These are all I could find." She handed them to Katrina.

"Thank you for being kind." Katrina turned to leave.

"I'm sorry sweetheart. It wasn't supposed to be like this. Get out of here as fast as you can."

Katrina ran back to the fight. James lifted the butt of a rifle and knocked out a guard. Dreya and Mia were tying another guard to the poles. No one was firing anymore. She let out a long whistle and held up the truck keys.

"Ethan!" Willow screamed as she dropped to the ground and lifted his limp body from the dirt.

"Help me carry him to the trucks," Becca called out. "We need to get out of here."

Katrina's eyes met with James'. He smiled at her and nodded. They did it, she thought, they actually freaking did it. Katrina smiled ear to ear as she turned to run to the trucks to get them started.

Once she cleared the tents, she saw a stream of headlights coming down the dirt road kicking up a field of dust in their yellow beams. Katrina turned to look back at James.

Lt. Bayer grabbed her by the neck and put his cold revolver against her temple. She quickly tossed the keys to Dreya. "Go!" Katrina screamed. "Go now!"

"Go where?" Lt. Bayer laughed. "You kids sure picked a bad night for an uprising. That's the new unit coming in right now to replace us. In a few seconds, there will be double the amount of guards here than on any other day. Silly girl." He pushed his forehead against Katrina's cheek. "I expected better from you," he whispered.

Katrina threw her head to the side to smack it into his face. He laughed as he rubbed his chin and tightened his grip on her neck until she passed out.

Chapter 23

Katrina came back to consciousness hearing Dreya scream at the guards. The kids were all zip tied to the main poles that held up the tent structure. Katrina tried to free her arms, but she couldn't move her shoulder.

"You can't control us," Dreya shouted. "You can't keep us locked up against our will. This isn't fair. We deserve a chance to decide our own fate!"

"You are getting the world handed to you on a silver platter little girl. Yet you are still complaining," a short man with greying hair said as he stood next to Lt. Bayer surrounded by a group of new guards. "I thought this dandelion gene thing made them passive and easy going."

"Well you got that wrong," Dreya spat. "Dandelions are weeds. You can't make us stop and you can't kill us. We are stronger than you."

Stop it, Dreya. Stop, stop, stop, Katrina thought as her head cleared.

"Is this the leader then?" the grey-haired guard said as he lifted her to her feet. "Get her out of here. She is someone else's problem now."

"No!" Mia screamed as they threw Dreya onto the ground and twisted her arms behind her back. "Leave my sister alone you assholes!" Mia struggled against her restraints. "Let me go. Let me go with her."

"Shut up," the grey-haired man pointed at Mia. "I'm done playing with you kids. Your sister chose her fate."

Dreya pushed her chin into the dirt on the ground to turn her head as she looked for Katrina. Once they secured her hands and feet, two men lifted her up. "Take care of her," Dreya whispered. Katrina nodded with tears in her eyes as they carried Dreya away to the trucks.

*

Katrina was fully alert as she looked around to the faces of the other kids sitting on the ground while tied to the poles. The flood lights under the tent illuminated the guards in the center. Ethan sat propped against the wall looking around. Across from them, half hidden in the dark, sat James staring at her. She watched the relief cross his face when he saw her focus on him.

Jayden was trying to reason with the guards. "You can't take her away sir. It was all of us that decided to act. There wasn't a central leader."

"Shut up kid," the grey hair man said.

"Listen…" Jayden pleaded.

"General Edwards told you to shut up," Lt. Bayer shouted. "Now is the time for you to listen." Jayden closed his mouth as he glared at Lt. Bayer. Mia's cries fell softer. The guards were released from the shelter and the rest of the new guards came marching over from their vehicles.

A tall man with auburn hair shaved close to his head and a blunt mustache came over with the group of replacement guards. He looked young, Katrina thought. And familiar. The man glanced briefly at Katrina and then turned his face forward again as he went walking by.

The moment their eyes met a hundred memories came rushing to her. Sitting in her dad's office, waiting for him to get done with a meeting. A young Marine at the front desk. Rock or Stone or Boulder. Corporal Boulder. He was a wounded war veteran, highly decorated, on a light duty assignment.

Two years he had been there. Waiting for her dad to give him an order. Taking messages, making calls. When she had gotten hurt in P.E. she talked to him on the phone. He had run into the meeting to pull her dad out so that he could come pick her up from school. Katrina felt sick to her stomach. She turned and vomited on the ground.

"Is this really happening?" General Edwards looked at her in disgust. "I guess it isn't babysitting duty without the tantrums and the throw up."

"That's Sgt. Major Floyd's daughter," Lt. Bayer said.

"You don't say?" The general rubbed his chin. "You'd figure she'd have a stronger gut."

Bayer laughed. "That's what I thought too."

Katrina stared at Mia and said nothing back to the men.

"Alright kids," General Edwards said. "Here are the new rules. You have lost all your privileges. No more movies, no more free time. Bed time is now 20:00 hours. No more meetings or gatherings in secret. There will be guards stationed down in the shelter twenty four hours a day. One will be posted outside each door to the rooms. Life is about to get a whole lot harder until you can prove to me that you can earn back my trust. Cut them free and get them back down there," he directed the men.

*

Mia crawled into her bed sobbing. Katrina walked over and awkwardly put her hand on Mia's hair.

"It's going to be alright." Katrina patted the girl's head. "We will find a way to get her back."

"How?" Mia choked out the word between broken sounds. "Your plans suck. How will we get her back?"

"Shhh," Katrina soothed as a guard crossed their room to stand by the tunnel door. "It'll be okay."

Mia cried herself to sleep and Katrina crawled into her bed exhausted from the night's events. She turned her head trying to get comfortable on the pillow and heard James tapping softly on the metal frame. He reached his hand up the side of the bed and Katrina leaned over to weave her fingers through his. She squeezed his hand and laid there in the dark with their fingers interlaced.

*

Katrina coaxed Mia out of bed the next morning and got her to the lesson. The guard outside the door escorted all of Room 3 to the common room. Dr. C's eyes were puffy and red, but she carried on with the lecture. Mia sat quietly in front of Katrina. Becca slid over next to them.

"We were so close," Becca whispered looking straight ahead. "I can't believe how close we were."

"I'm sorry," Katrina whispered back. She stared down at Mia's slouching shoulders. "I wish I would have made us wait or something."

"It's not your fault," Becca sighed. "How could you have known? We will try again."

Katrina said nothing as she looked at Mia's back.

"You girls," a guard snapped from the side of the bleachers, "separate now." Becca put her hands up and scooted away from Katrina. Dr. C kept talking.

Chapter 24

Outside privileges had been revoked. The guards ran the kids in circles around the common room until Katrina's heart wanted to jump out of her chest. She stayed by Mia's side through the run. James and Jayden kept right behind them. When Mia slowed down around a turn, a guard yelled at her to go faster. Mia glared at the man as she took off at full speed leaving Katrina, James, and Jayden to catch up.

More guards came down after the exercise session and stood inspecting the kids as they cleaned the entire shelter from top to bottom. By the time the dinner packets arrived, Katrina was a new level of exhausted. She fell onto the floor beside James and devoured her entire meal.

Mia barely touched her food. Jayden sat with her and kept encouraging her to eat. After dinner, General Edwards had all the kids gather in the common room.

"This is what every day will look like until I feel you all have learned your lesson. The minute one of you steps out of line, we start back over from the beginning." Katrina looked over to see Willow staring at her. She gave her a small smile and Willow turned back to face the general. "I expect you all to show your gratitude for this world we are working so hard to build for you."

*

When the fluorescent lights came on in the morning the guards switched duty with new ones. Katrina watched in disgust as Corporal Boulder took his post by the tunnel door.

"What are you even doing here?" she asked him as she pulled the breakfast packs out from the cabinet. "How could you betray your country like this? And where is my dad?" She slammed the cabinet shut.

Cpl. Boulder looked straight ahead with a peculiar smile playing on his face. "Hurry up and eat, kid. You don't want to be late," he said.

"Are you kidding me?" Katrina threw the food packets on the floor. "You don't even have the decency to answer me."

"Do we have a problem?" The guard by the exit put his hand on his rifle.

Ethan hobbled over to pick up the food packs as James pulled Katrina to their bunk.

"No problem sir," James smiled. "She just gets crabby when she is hungry."

"Well eat. Then get moving." The guard relaxed his hand.

"What's the matter with you?" James whispered as he opened a packet and handed it to her.

Katrina bit her bottom lip. "I know that guy," she whispered. "He worked for my dad."

James looked to Cpl. Boulder and then back to her. "Does he still work for your dad?" Katrina shrugged.

"Eat," the second guard snapped. "You are going to be late."

*

They finished breakfast and started walking down the hall. Cpl. Boulder was escorting them, but he stopped halfway through the tunnel and pulled Katrina back. "Keep moving," he directed the others. James hesitated but Katrina nodded to him, so he kept walking.

"Don't do anything stupid and don't say anything stupid," Cpl. Boulder whispered. Katrina turned to glare at him but stayed silent. "Your dad sent me here to get you out."

Katrina's heart skipped a beat. "Is he… okay?" she stuttered.

Cpl. Boulder's lip raised. "Of course he is okay. Did you think he wouldn't be?"

"I don't know what to think anymore," she said as she crossed her arms.

"Well don't think then," Boulder said as he started walking.

"Wait," Katrina held him back. "Tell me why. Why are you guys shooting civilians? Why did you turn against your country? How could you do it?"

Cpl. Boulder chuckled. "You've got that all wrong."

"Enlighten me then."

"Your dad has been trying to warn us all along. No one listened to him. It's too late now."

"So now you are just following orders?" Katrina rolled her eyes.

"There is more to the story than you know, and I don't have time to explain it all right now," Cpl. Boulder sighed. "Just be ready to go when I tell you."

Katrina watched as Jayden put his arm around Mia to protectively guide her into the common room. James looked back to her just as he was exiting the tunnel. She smiled at him. "I'm not leaving without them."

"I said don't be stupid." Boulder grabbed her good shoulder. "Those aren't the orders I was given."

Katrina pushed his hand away. "I don't care what your orders are. I don't leave without my friends. You'll have to find a way to make that happen if you want me to go." They were nearing the end of the hall.

"And what am I supposed to tell your dad?"

"Tell him that I fell in love." Katrina's lip curled into a half smile.

"I did tell you not to say anything stupid." Boulder ran his hand over his face. Katrina laughed as she walked out of the tunnel and went to sit with the rest of Room 3.

*

The same recording as the previous two days played on the screen. Dr. C wasn't there for the class that morning. In her place, an elderly man with large ears and a long chin stood uncomfortably in front of the bleachers. Ethan was allowed to skip gentleman class while his ribs healed so he sat with the health class.

The man cleared his throat. "Good morning students, I am Mr. Wilkson. Today we are going to cover infant CPR. This is important so pay attention."

Ethan raised his hand. "I have a question. Why don't we learn survival anymore?"

Mr. Wilkson chuckled. "Well son, you won't need it. That was just a precaution put in place by a very influential man. There was no telling the damage all those nuclear explosions would do so he wanted you to be prepared in case you would be all alone. Turns out, you don't need it. We are here to guide you and protect you now. As long as you play by the rules you won't have to worry about anything."

"I have another question." Mia raised her hand. "Where is Dr. C? Why isn't she here teaching us?"

The vein on Mr. Wilkson's neck bulged. "She was deemed unfit to guide you," he said. "Let's begin."

"Wait." Mia sat up straighter. "Where is she?"

Lark sighed loudly from across the bleachers as he turned to face Mia. "How about you let Mr. Wilkson get on with teaching the class, princess?"

Mia started to stand up and Katrina pulled her back down to sitting. "Look straight ahead," she whispered into Mia's ear. "Don't respond."

Lt. Bayer came walking over to the bleachers. "Is there a problem here?" he asked.

Lark smiled. "Why don't you ask Room 3?"

"Ah. My wayward children," Lt. Bayer said as he walked over to Katrina. "Not causing any trouble, I hope. We can always go see General Edwards if you like." His teeth reflected the harsh lights as he stared into Katrina's eyes.

She lowered her head. "Nope. No problem here," she whispered. James tensed beside her, but she pressed her leg against his until she felt him relax, long after Lt. Bayer walked away.

Chapter 25

Ethan laid in bed with a headache during dinner. When General Edward called them to the common room before bedtime, Ethan was already asleep.

Mia climbed into her bunk. "I'm not going. I don't feel good either." She pulled the blanket over her head.

"Mia," Jayden said pulling the blanket back. "We need to keep playing by the rules for a while. You can do this."

Katrina walked up beside him. "Come on sweetheart. This won't take long hopefully."

Cpl. Boulder yelled over to the guard by the exit. "Daniels escort these boys to the common room. I'm going to get the doctor."

The young guard jumped up and ran over to the door. "Let's go," he shouted to James and Jayden.

Katrina looked at Cpl. Boulder as he walked away from the door. "She is fine. She just doesn't want to go."

"You look sick too kid," Cpl. Boulder stared at her. "Better get into bed." James looked back to Katrina as Daniels pushed him and Jayden out of the room.

Katrina turned to Cpl. Boulder in confusion and then her heart started to pound as his actions began to make sense. "Not without them," she whispered. "All of them or I don't go."

"Listen," Cpl. Boulder pulled her to the exit. "I radioed your dad earlier. He said the girl comes too. That's all I can do." He stopped by the door. "Mia," he called. "Come with us to see the doctor."

Mia climbed down from her bunk. "I'm not really sick," her voice trailed off as she saw the look on Boulder's face.

Katrina stood her ground. "Fine then. Take Mia somewhere safe. Take her to my dad. But I'm not leaving without the rest of my roommates."

Cpl. Boulder groaned as he stared at Katrina. "Ethan, get up," he yelled.

"I'm already up." Ethan turned to face them with bloodshot eyes. "Go without me."

"You'll be okay buddy," Katrina reassured him. "We are going somewhere safe."

"I'm sure it is safe." Ethan put his hand over his eyes. "But I can't leave. Willow is here. She needs me."

Katrina's voice caught in her throat and she coughed to clear it. "I'm going to find a way to get the rest of you out."

"I know you will, but for now get Mia out of here." He turned his face back toward the wall. Cpl. Boulder pushed Mia and Katrina up the dirt steps.

"I'm serious." Katrina pushed herself against the wall of earth. "I'm not leaving without James and Jayden."

"I know," Cpl. Boulder said pushing her up the next step. "I heard you. First let me get you to the truck and I'll figure out the rest."

Katrina inhaled deeply as she stepped onto the surface and away from the tunnel. The red sun was starting to set behind the mountains in the west. Grey streaks of fog still filled the sky but blue, the weakest shades of blue, began to filter through. Night would be here soon, Katrina smiled to herself. Another day would come and another gust of wind and another moment for the earth to heal.

"Where are you taking those kids?" A solider called from under the tent.

"To medical, Sergeant." Cpl. Boulder snapped to attention. "They are coming down with something."

"Get moving then Corporal. We've got to take care of our livestock." The sergeant laughed as he walked away. Boulder pushed the girls further into the tent behind a screened off room.

"This isn't the plan," Boulder whispered to Katrina. "Just play along. We are improvising." Mia grabbed Katrina's hand as they stepped into the medical section.

The doctor was a tall, thin man with strawberry blond hair. His arms and face were dotted with freckles. He stood hunched over and leaned against a table with his arms crossed. Dr. C was sitting in the chair talking with him. Her eyes lit up when she saw Mia and Katrina enter.

"What is going on Corporal?" The doctor addressed Boulder.

Katrina stepped forward. "We don't feel so hot."

"Well let me take a look at you," the doctor said taking his stethoscope off his neck.

"Um, actually," Mia said while eyeing the device. "It's more along the line of girl problems." The doctor flushed as he turned to Dr. C. She covered a giggle with a cough as she stood up.

"Why don't you let me handle this one John?" Dr. C nodded toward the door. John began to walk out and motioned for Boulder to follow.

"One second doc," he said, and John quickly left the room.

"Go get them," Katrina said to Boulder. His jaw dropped open as he looked to Dr. C and then back to Katrina. "We can trust her." She crossed her arms over her chest. "Now please find a way to get James and Jayden out." Boulder sighed as he ran out of the tent.

"What's going on if you don't mind me asking?" Dr. C guided Mia and Katrina to sit on the patient bed.

"I just don't feel good." Mia glared at her. "This place sucks and I want my sister back."

"You poor sweethearts." She went to grab them each a water bottle. "I am so sorry that you have to go through this." When Dr. C turned to the light, Katrina saw the bruise on her cheek that she had tried to hide with makeup.

"What did they do to you?" Katrina asked as she took the bottle.

Dr. C's hand fluttered to her face. "Oh. Nothing. Please don't worry about me, I'll be fine." She smiled at the girls.

Katrina shook her head. "None of this is fine. Why is this even happening?"

"I don't know honey. None of this is what was supposed to happen. They called us all up, all the active duty military, right before the bombs went off. We should have known that they knew about it. How else could they have planned this far in advance? Except, the orders didn't seem right. We hunkered down the first two days and then we were given MOPP suits to withstand the radiation. They mobilized us shortly after, sending various units out on missions. I was sent to a holding facility in Fallon, Nevada to provide medical care to patients that never came."

Katrina nodded. "We were there. They kept us for a few days when we got captured on the mountain. A woman with a high bun was nice to us, the colonel not so much."

"That was probably Vivian. Colonel Adams is a little rough. The food there was just awful wasn't it?" Dr. C put her hand on her mouth.

Katrina smiled. "It wasn't so bad. We each got an apple."

"An apple sounds delicious right now." Dr. C returned her smile. "Anyway. Sometime in the second week they took away our uniforms and replaced them with these green jumpsuits. Then they took down the flags. I should have known then, but it was all so confusing. We couldn't call anyone, and we had no news. Three weeks in there was a rumor that military members were deserting because they didn't want to follow orders. They were being told to wipe out the survivors. To go into the bunkers and get rid of those who lived."

Tears began to roll down Dr. C's cheeks. "That day they told me I was being reassigned to

Project Dandelion. They said you kids were the hope for the new world and that you needed us here to protect you. I was happy to come, but now… Now I don't know what to think." Mia had pulled her knees to her chest and stared through Dr. C with a vacant look in her eyes.

Katrina took Dr. C's hand in her own. "We are getting out," she whispered. "The corporal is going back for Jayden and James and then we are getting out of here. Will you help us?"

Dr. C dried her tears with the corner of her sleeve and then tilted her chin up. "I don't know what I can do but I will do whatever you need me to do."

Katrina hugged her. "Right now, we just need to sit here and wait."

*

Katrina stared at the ground as Dr. C went to tell John the girls needed to lie down for a little while. The earth floor was broken in, pounded flat by the foot prints and equipment that had stamped over it in the past few weeks. She felt numb staring at it and smirked to herself when she recognized the emotion. They all had been numb, she thought. Distant and removed, not caring enough to actually do anything to stop this. What could she have done though?

"I'm scared," Mia whispered, breaking Katrina's trance. "What if I never see Dreya again?"

Katrina looked at the girl and smiled. "I promise we will find your sister."

"How can you promise something like that though?" Mia moved closer to her. "What if she comes back here looking for me? Where are we even going?"

"It's my dad getting us out." Katrina looked at the partition that Dr. C had walked behind. Nothing moved. "I'll ask him to help us find her. He will help."

Mia covered her eyes with her hand and then slid her palm down her face. "But your dad helped to build all of this. He is in the military. How can we trust him?"

"I don't know anything anymore. I don't know why or how this happened. No one felt like telling us the whole truth at first because they thought we were a bunch of dumb kids. Or maybe they did, and we just didn't listen. That doesn't matter anymore now. My gut tells me to trust my dad. He left the truck to help me get out. That has to count for something right?"

Mia hugged her knees to her chest again and was silent for a moment. "She trusted you, so I'll trust you too. But if this turns out to be another bad plan, well I told you so."

Katrina smiled. "It is the only one we have right now. And sometimes you just have to hope."

Chapter 26

"Stand up and put your hands behind your back," Cpl. Boulder commanded as he stepped into the medical area. Katrina jumped to her feet. Mia was shaking beside her.

"What is the meaning of this?" Dr. C yelled as she ran into the room. "These girls are sick. You brought them in here for help."

"I'm under new orders," Cpl. Boulder said as he secured zip ties around their wrists. They were military grade ties, heavy duty. Katrina panicked. I don't know if I can break this one, she thought.

"What's going on?" Mia cried out. "You can't just keep tying us up for no reason." Cpl. Boulder stared hard into Katrina's eyes as he finished securing Mia's hands.

Her heart slowed down, and her vision cleared. "Do what he says Mia. We have to trust that it will be okay." Mia stopped talking but she was still shaking.

"What is happening?" John asked as he walked into the tent.

"This man," Dr. C pointed at Boulder, "is harassing our young women patients and tying them up."

"I'm under new orders sir," Cpl. Boulder addressed John. "I'm to take them to a different dandelion unit. They want all the trouble makers removed to there."

"These girls are not trouble makers," Dr. C put her foot down. "They are very well behaved."

"I'm sorry ma'am." Cpl. Boulder grabbed Katrina by the arm. "Orders are orders. I promise they will be taken care of though."

"We will be okay," Katrina whispered to Dr. C as she was led out of the room. "Thank you for everything." Dr. C stood back with John and watched the girls leave.

*

Jayden and James stood just outside the tents with their arms also tied. Katrina had to wipe the smile from her cheeks as she saw James and then looked back to Boulder's stone face. She stared at her feet as they moved forward, the happiness bubbling inside of her. He did it, she thought. This guy is a superhero. Cpl. Boulder had them stand in line and began to march them to the vehicle.

"And where do you think you are all going?" Lt. Bayer's voice came from the shadows. He stepped out under the floodlights illuminating the outskirts of the tents.

Cpl. Boulder halted the kids. "I have orders from the higher ups. These kids have been labeled as instigators, so they are being moved to another shelter. I'm to bring you back replacements."

"And how did you receive this order?" Lt. Bayer stood a few inches shorter than Boulder. He widened his stance and crossed his arms to make up for it.

"Sgt. Major Floyd radioed a few minutes ago. General Edwards spoke with him. Ask the general if you have any questions sir," Cpl. Boulder said looking past Bayer.

"Why do you think Floyd would send his own daughter to the bad kid's shelter?" Lt. Bayer scratched his chin.

Mia's eyes widened as she looked to Katrina for an answer. Katrina stomped gently on Mia's foot and she looked back to the ground.

"I don't know sir. Maybe you should ask the Sgt. Major that question."

Lt. Bayer looked to the night sky for a moment before he burst out laughing. "I'm just giving you grief man." He lightly punched Boulder's shoulder. "I already talked to General Edwards. He told me to ride along with you to see if I could be of any assistance."

Cpl. Boulder's lips twitched into a forced smile. "Thank you sir, but I'll be okay. I don't need any assistance."

Lt. Bayer shrugged. "Orders are orders, corporal. Let's get this show on the road."

*

Cpl. Boulder led the kids into the back of an enclosed camper military truck. Lt. Bayer shut the tailgate and winked at Katrina before walking over to the passenger side. James was bouncing his knee with his tongue in his cheek. Katrina slid over to sit next to him.

"Are you okay?" she whispered.

"I hate that guy," James hissed back. "I hate his whole family. How are we going to get out of this one?"

"I don't know." Katrina shook her head. "I'm hoping Boulder has a plan. Did you hear him talking to my dad?"

"No," James said as he looked out the back window. "He brought the radio to General Edwards during his speech. The general walked away to take the call. He looked scared when he came back and told us to go with Boulder."

Katrina smiled. "Yeah. My dad has that effect."

"Listen." James turned to look at Katrina. "I'm trusting you, trusting your dad, because I think I love you."

"Or you just don't have another option." Katrina smiled at him, butterflies flipping in her stomach.

"Something like that." James leaned his head back against the metal wall of the camper.

"Wait," Katrina said as the truck roared to life. "Did you just say you love me?" Cpl. Boulder pulled the truck out of the compound entrance and stared driving down the dirt road.

"Yeah," James sighed. "I guess I did."

Katrina's smile spread across her face. She adjusted her hands up higher against her back so she could lean over and kiss James on the cheek. "I think I love you too," she whispered. "But only kind of. Don't get a big head."

Chapter 27

They drove through the night. James stretched his legs out and Katrina laid her head on his lap. Mia curled up behind Katrina's bent knees and used her thigh as a pillow. Jayden sat up on the other side of Mia, keeping her warm and talking with James until they both fell asleep.

Katrina could feel Mia's even breathing as she slept. It's going to be okay, she told herself. I'm going to see my dad. And if it's the worst-case scenario, if he helped to destroy and create this world, I'll convince him he was brainwashed. He'll let me, let us, go to the cabin. I know it. And somehow, I'll convince him to help me find Dreya too. It's all going to be okay, she thought again as she drifted off to sleep to the rhythmic humming of the truck driving through the desert.

*

Daylight came filtering through the dirty window in the back of the truck as Cpl. Boulder pulled over to the side of the road.

"Wake up kids," Lt. Bayer called while banging on the side of the truck. "Time for a pit stop."

Katrina groaned as she sat up and tried to rotate her stiff shoulders. Her hands were tingling below where the zip tie was placed, and her hip ached from laying on the metal floor. Cpl. Boulder opened the back of the truck and the kids climbed down.

She was just about to slide out when Boulder grabbed her by the wrists. He cut her zip tie loose with a single slice and put the pocket knife into her hands. "Wait a second," he whispered in her ear.

Cpl. Boulder stepped to the side of the truck, standing in front of the kids. Lt. Bayer stood in the brush with his back to the truck facing the rising sun.

"Bayer," Cpl. Boulder shouted, raising his pistol toward him. "Put your hands in the air and then turn around."

Lt. Bayer put his hands in the air as he slowly turned. His face was distorted in confusion. "What do you think you are doing? Corporal? Lower your weapon now. That is an order."

Boulder chuckled. "An order from who? You? You aren't my chain of command and I don't take orders from pansies like you. Katrina, take his gun." Katrina ran over to unholster the pistol from Bayer's waist. "Drop to your knees now Bayer. Kids, get back in the truck." Boulder held his pistol out, trained steadily on the man's head.

"This isn't the last I will be seeing of you sweetheart," Bayer whispered to Katrina. "I have a feeling that our paths will cross again. Say hi to your dad for me, will you?" He smiled at her and Katrina's stomach rolled as she quickly ran back to the truck. She kept the gun pressed tightly against her as she climbed back in. Boulder's arm holding the pointed pistol didn't waver as he walked over to the driver's side and started the vehicle.

"It would probably be best if you shot me Corporal," Bayer called out.

"It probably would be," Boulder yelled back as he stepped onto the frame. "But I don't shoot unarmed people." He slid into the seat and slammed on the gas pedal. The truck went screeching down the desert road.

*

They traveled deeper into the desert over bumpy dirt roads. Joshua Trees began to sprout up and a random cactus or two poked out straight from the ground. The air was hot and stifling in the back of the truck. Katrina wished she could open a window. They drove past abandoned houses and stores down a long, paved road. The truck slowed as it moved between concrete barrier slabs.

"Where are we going?" Mia asked trying to look out of the back window.

"It's some kind of military base I think." Katrina moved to sit next to her. "We are coming up to the gate." Boulder stopped the truck as he talked to the gate guards before driving through the station.

They passed three Marines and a Sailor holding rifles at the entrance.

Outside of the back window, Katrina saw the giant flag poles inside the barricaded walls surrounding the base. All four branches of the military flags flew beside the Marine flag along with a yellow Gadsden "don't tread on me" flag depicting the coiled snake. The flags were all flown at half-mast slightly beneath the American flag. The American flag was hung upside down signifying the country in distress. Katrina felt a rush of pride tainted with sadness as she watched the fabric dance in the wind.

Chapter 28

The truck climbed a small hill up to a circular driveway which sat in front of a cluster of buildings. Boulder pulled to the end of the circle and killed the engine. He jumped out and ran to open the tailgate.

Mia climbed out first and momentarily disappeared from Katrina's line of vision. She heard the girl scream "Dreya!" at the top of her lungs and Katrina scrambled out after her.

Running down the steps from the center building was Dreya. Her braid, with all its flyaways, was blowing in the desert breeze. The hot air burned Katrina's eyes and dried the tears that began to form as she watched Mia tackle her older sister to the pavement.

Katrina looked to Jayden who had quickly climbed out of the truck when he heard Mia scream. "What are you waiting for?" she laughed. "Go get your girl."

"Nah." Jayden smiled as he put his hands in his pockets. "Let them have this moment. I'll get her later."

Katrina smiled as she turned to James and he kissed the top of her head. When she looked back to the girls, she saw a tall Marine with wide shoulders and tightly shaved hair cut exit the main building. The

Marine made his way down the steps. Katrina thought of all the times her father had deployed and how it had seemed that every Marine in uniform looked like him. But this time... She sharply inhaled.

"Daddy," she called out leaving James' embrace and running to her father. He opened his arms wide and caught her in a crushing bear hug.

"It's so good to see you sweetie," he said putting her down on her feet. "I'm really glad you are okay."

"Um." Katrina took a step back and glared at him as the words rushed out of her mouth. "No thanks to you! Well maybe right this minute and the truck, thanks for that by the way, but what the hell is going on? Why did you put me in that bunker? Why did you leave me there? You lied to me! You told me you didn't know what was going on with the bombs. What is this new government and why is the military shooting unarmed civilians? I want answers and I want them now. Starting with, how could you do this to me?"

Sgt. Major Floyd let out a deep chested laugh as he ruffled the top of his daughter's head. "It's good to see that even the apocalypse didn't change your attitude, I guess. I told you the truth. You were safe there while I did what I needed to do. If it's any consolation, I blew my cover due to the stunt you pulled back at the shelter, so we lost an edge in this war. I was already going to get the sister out- I like

Dreya by the way, you could take some lessons in manners from her- but you had to throw a tantrum and cause a scene."

More men in service uniforms came out and Boulder went to them. "Sgt. Major," he yelled. "The Corpsmen want to take a look at the kids."

"In a minute," Sgt. Major Floyd called back. He looked to his daughter. "We saw this coming and we tried to warn them. I could have left. I probably should have left. But there were some good people caught up in all the confusion. I couldn't leave my men behind."

"What is this then?" Katrina asked looking around the base. "Are you working for the new world government?"

Her dad smiled his big lopsided grin. "Those bunch of traitors? Hell no." He spread his arms out wide. "Welcome to the resistance."

He crossed his arms back over his chest as Katrina's jaw dropped. "So, we are fighting the government now?"

"Not my government," Sgt. Major Floyd said. "We weren't going down with those fascists, so we did our job as we formed the resistance under the radar. This new government thought we were just sheep, but we are wolves dressed in wool. Thinking that we were weak and would follow their rules was their first mistake. We've taken back most of the military bases around the country and more are joining us every day. We sure as hell weren't going down without a fight. And oh, what a fight we are going to give them."

Katrina hugged her dad again. "I knew it wasn't true. All the stuff they were saying about you."

Her dad smiled. "You can tell me all about that later. And I really want to know why you weren't at the cabin. Cpl. Boulder was supposed to meet you up there before we got word that you were captured by Colonel Adams." He chuckled. "I've been sending that poor kid all up and down the state looking for you. Maybe you should thank him sometime, eh?"

"Maybe you should thank him." Katrina narrowed her eyes. "You were the one giving him orders."

"Ah, he volunteered for it." Sgt. Major Floyd put his arm over his daughter's shoulders. "Introduce me to your friends."

Dreya and Mia were standing by James and Jayden near the truck. Katrina squeezed her dad's hands as they neared her roommates. Jayden tucked a lock of Dreya's wild hair behind her ear and smiled at her with adoring eyes.

"You already met Dreya," Katrina said as they approached. "How did that happen by the way?"

Her dad nodded. "I heard of a rebel leader in the mix, she belonged here."

Katrina shook her head. "Well this is her little sister Mia, and this is Jayden, her boyfriend."

Jayden shook the Sgt. Major's hand. "It's nice to meet you."

"Likewise," Sgt. Major Floyd smiled at him. "I've heard a lot about you."

Mia grabbed Sgt. Major Floyd's waist and crushed him with a hug. "Thank you so much for saving my sister and for getting us out of that awful place."

"Now, now," Katrina's dad smiled at her. "Don't go thanking me just yet. We still have some work to do and I will need every able body to accomplish the mission."

Mia stood up straight. "Whatever you need me to do sir, I'm your girl."

Katrina laughed as she turned her dad away. "And this," she said smiling as she raised her chin. "Daddy, this is James."

James extended his hand. Katrina saw it shake and hoped her dad wouldn't notice. "Thank you for getting us out sir."

Sgt. Major Floyd looked up and down over James. "Uh huh," he mumbled, leaving James' hand hanging in the air. He turned to face the buildings. "Let's get you kids inside. It is hot as hell out here." He began to walk away, and the teens trailed behind him.

Mia and Dreya laughed as they teased one another. Jayden couldn't wipe the smile from his face. He kept glancing over to look at Dreya as if he was worried that she wasn't real. James and Katrina followed them across the pavement and onto the sidewalk.

"I'm not so sure your dad likes me," James whispered to her as they climbed the stairs.

"Of course he does," Katrina smiled. "He doesn't have another choice."

If you like *Project Dandelion: Reentry*, please consider leaving a review! Indie authors can't survive without word of mouth referrals from readers like you.

Follow the author on Instagram and Facebook @Heathercarsonauthor

Or visit

www.heatherkcarson.com

Made in the USA
Middletown, DE
12 November 2019